TOYING

KYLIE GILMORE

Toying: © 2021 by Kylie Gilmore

Cover design by: Michele Catalano Creative

Published by: Extra Fancy Books

ISBN-13: 978-1-64658-027-9

Get ready for a thunderbolt!

1

Sloane

Just call me an odd duck. So what if I'm having a drink at my hometown bar alone on a Saturday night? I take a sip of black and tan, feeling more conspicuous than usual with the crowd here tonight. Seems like I stumbled upon a Robinson family reunion or something. The Robinsons have owned and operated The Horseman Inn, a historic bar and restaurant in town, for generations. But this is epic proportions of Robinsons, who seem to have multiplied while I was away. It's the Saturday after Thanksgiving, so they probably needed to get out of the house after all that feasting, touch football games, and whatever the hell else big happy families do. I wouldn't know. It's been just me and Dad for a long time.

A guy in his thirties with slick blond hair at the other end of the bar catches my eye, lifting a hand in a small wave. My pulse kicks up. No wedding band, and he's cute. I don't know him from growing up.

I wave back and feel my cheeks flush. *Chill!* I take a cooling sip of my drink, hoping he'll approach. I'm not good at flirting. You'd think I'd be great at it, considering I've only ever had guy friends. I get how their minds work. Unfortunately, most guys see me as a buddy or someone to help with their car. I'm a mechanic.

I shouldn't get my hopes up. Good-looking guys never try to pick me up in a bar. Or anywhere, really. Usually the way I get with a guy is simple—one of my guy friends gets horny and makes a move on me. I'm convenient. Then we're not friends anymore because things get weird after sex with a friend. Most of those hookups fizzle out in two weeks tops.

I no longer attempt to make my own move on cute guys after the mortifying time I approached a guy at a bar, who I thought was giving me an interested look and, taking a cue from my guy friends, I told him I was feeling off until he turned me on. Yeah, I went there. In my defense, I'd seen it work successfully many times for my friends. That so back-fired. He asked me if I was actually a guy who dressed like a girl. He then pulled my hair to see if it was a wig. So *that* happened. All of which is to say it's no surprise I've had zero relationships that last longer than two weeks, which sucks because I'd really like to have a serious relationship.

The cute guy from across the bar makes his move and takes the empty stool next to me. I'm more than a little excited to be picked up in a bar. It's flattering and ripe with potential. He's dressed nice in a denim shirt and jeans. "Hey, I'm Brad."

I smile, tucking my hair behind my ears. "Sloane."

"Don't you work over at Murray's?"

"Yup." Murray's is Dad's auto repair shop in town.

He flashes a pearly white smile. "Female mechanic, huh? That's hot."

I appreciate the hot part, just not enough to cancel out the rest. "I prefer to be called a mechanic, not a *female* mechanic."

"Touchy."

I frown. Damn right I'm touchy. I've never felt accepted by family or the outside world for loving being a mechanic. Screw them. Dad's shop is the only place I've ever felt at home. This guy needs enlightening. "What do you do for a living?"

"Stockbroker."

"Do people ever call you a male stockbroker?"

He shifts closer. "Feisty, I like it. Listen, I've got the

Mercedes-Benz out front. It's making this weird noise when I accelerate. Let's go for a drive so you can take a listen and tell me what's wrong with it."

My cheeks burn with humiliation. Why did I get my hopes up that a cute guy is actually interested in me? I'm no beauty, and I know it. I'm short, flat chested, and slim hipped. No busty curves like most guys want. I've also got straight shoulder-length brown hair and a plain face. Tonight I'm wearing a long-sleeved white cotton shirt with black yoga pants. The height of fashion. Not.

I pull a business card from my small purse. "Here. Call the shop on Monday morning for an appointment." I'm hoping to be partner at Murray's one day, and that's not going to happen if I'm giving away business, always helping people with their cars in my free time. I have to prove to Dad I can build the client list. It's not a sure thing I'll be partner even then. Dad and I are in a standoff over my job situation there.

Brad takes the card and shoves it in his back pocket. "Thanks." He lowers his voice. "You into girls, Sloane? That could be hot."

Wow, so glad he finds so many things about me hot. Small-minded people like him regularly make judgments about me because of my job. Not that there's anything wrong with being gay. I just don't think you should label someone because their gender doesn't fit what you think belongs with their job. I wouldn't assume a guy who worked in a female-dominated field like preschool education was gay just because of his job. Everyone should do the job best suited to them. Period.

I meet his gaze directly. "Funny you should ask. I'm waiting for my girlfriend to get back from the restroom. You can go now."

He gives me a sly smile. "I'd be into that. How about the three of us go for a drive?"

"How about you go back to that rock you slithered out from under?"

"Bitch."

He swaggers back to the other end of the bar and then talks to his friend while looking at me, probably filling him in on the bitch. I press my lips together in a flat line. What a jerk. I can't believe I got excited for a minute there when he first approached.

I stay put, not ready to go home and face Dad's pointed questions about my job prospects. I quit my job as a high school math teacher last summer after four years of teaching. I've been home five months, working at Dad's shop, and haven't sent out a single job application because I don't want to work anywhere else. He doesn't seem to hear me when I tell him how much I want to stay, to be a bigger part of things at Murray's. He won't even let me do the books because he doesn't want me getting too involved when Murray's is supposed to be only a brief stop on the way to a better career.

Dad's super proud that I'm the first one in our family to go to college, and insists I need a job using my degree. Just to keep the peace, I told him I was sending out resumés, but nothing panned out yet. He's big on me using my degree because he was forced to drop out of high school and take over at Murray's to support his family when his dad died unexpectedly of a heart attack. I get where he's coming from; he missed out with no choice. But his no-choice career is my career of choice. Like I said, standoff.

The back dining room gets quiet. I glance over my shoulder. Eli Robinson stopped playing acoustic guitar. Jenna, his girlfriend, is sitting right up front, gazing adoringly at him. I fixed their cars after a minor fender bender.

I turn back to my drink. A few minutes later, a cheer goes up in the back dining room. I look over. It seems Eli and Jenna just got engaged. They were ahead of me in school, so I don't know them well. Even so, a lump of emotion lodges in my throat, seeing Jenna laughing and crying at the same time. Their family and friends surround them with hugs and cheerful congratulations. Big happy family. After Mom left, being an only child felt even lonelier. I used to fantasize about being part of a large family—brothers to hang with, sisters to teach me all that stuff girls seem to intuitively know. One day I hope to have a big family of my own, and then I'll never be on the outside again.

Right. I turn away, swiping an X with my finger through the condensation on my glass. I just need to find a guy who doesn't take one look at me and think "buddy" or "free auto repair." Guess I can add "threesome" to that list after tonight.

Since I've always had guy friends, I'm not the least intimidated to talk to guys, so a moment later when I overhear a guy say about his newly adopted dog, "Only love I have is for Huckleberry," I feel compelled to respond. *Huckleberry? Seriously?*

I turn, zeroing in on Caleb Robinson—male model—surrounded by women. Naturally. He's like the golden sun that women revolve around. There's no denying his male beauty. He's exquisite from his perfect angular cheekbones and square jaw to his well-formed muscular body. Greek god comes to mind.

"At least call him Huck," I say. "The other dogs will make fun of him for such a goofy name."

Oh shit! He's coming over.

I barely resist smoothing my hair. Have I learned nothing from tonight's events? Guys like him are never interested in girls like me. This time I really will be chill. Hopes are officially zero.

He ambles over, confidence personified, a small smile playing over his sensual lips.

My pulse races, and I brace myself for impact. I'm not even on the same playing field as Caleb. He's only here to defend his dog's ridiculous name.

He leans against the bar next to me. He's sporting a biker look—black leather jacket over a snug gray thermal with black jeans and black motorcycle boots. It's an odd contrast to his clean-cut good looks. His sandy brown hair is in a buzz cut, emphasizing the sharp angles of his clean-shaven face. Somehow he pulls it off.

He flashes a smile that sends an unexpected jolt through

me. He's even more good looking in person than the camera captures. And, believe me, that is *not* always the case. I know the modeling world. Mom put me through it as a kid until I aged out of my cuteness and fell face-first into awkwardness. A photographer told Mom in a stage whisper, which I heard loud and clear, that I was the ugly duckling in reverse, starting out adorable and then…not. He said I should just stop; no one would want to hire me anymore. Mom didn't defend me; instead she studied me critically and then looked resigned. I was twelve. I ruthlessly push down the horrendous memories of what followed that even now make me feel sick.

Caleb dips his head close to my ear. "I said, do you have a problem with the name Huckleberry?"

I snap to attention. "Come on, what kind of name is that for a dog?"

"An appropriate one. He's a Huckleberry." He holds my gaze for a long moment. "You're Sloane, right? From Murray's?"

Please don't say you need me to check out your car.

I really can't handle two guys in a row asking for a car consultation on a Saturday night. It would be an all-time low for me. Some part of me likes to keep the fantasy alive that I'll have a guy to settle down with one day for that big family I've always wanted.

I play it cool, turning the subject away from me and cars. "Yeah, I know who you are. Caleb Robinson. I've seen a few of your ads."

"Cool. I remember you from school. You were a year ahead of me. Eli mentioned you moved back to town."

I nod and turn back to my black and tan, taking a sip. Hopes remain at zero, which is fine. There's nothing more to say anyway. His dog has a goofy name, and he stands by it. I'm certainly not going to ask him about his modeling career. That's the world that chewed me up and spit me out.

"Hope you don't mind if I hang here a bit," he says. "My sister had this scary look of determination in her eyes as she headed straight for me. I got the feeling she was about to do some matchmaking. She tried to set up Eli before, and I fear I'm next."

I turn to him. "What if she picked out someone great?"

He shudders. "No, thanks. I like to keep my sister out of my personal life. She can be *relentless*. Don't get me wrong, I love her. She's like a second mom to me, but I'm an adult now, ya know?" Everyone in town heard about his mom dying in a car accident when we were kids. His big sister, Sydney, would naturally want to look out for him.

But as I glance up at six feet plus of muscled man, there's no question he's a full-grown adult. My throat goes dry. "Yup."

"Let me buy you a drink while I'm here."

I stare at my half-full glass. "I have a drink."

He chuckles. "So you do. I'll get your next one."

Before I can reply, he shares with no prompting from me about how Jenna and Eli almost didn't get together because Sydney didn't approve on account of Jenna's previous history of breaking guys' hearts with her lack of relationship skills. He sounds very mature and knowledgeable about relationships. An inkling of hope sneaks in.

"You sound like you have experience with relationships," I say.

"Not really." He chuckles. "Not at all. It's like the more a woman chases me, the less interested I am. And they always chase."

Zero hope. Zilch. Null set.

"Of course they do," I say blandly.

He smiles, shaking his head. "That sounded arrogant. I swear I'm not."

"Uh-huh."

He looks thoughtful, his eyes intent on mine. "I guess the right woman never came along."

"No beautiful models crossed your path?"

"I didn't say that."

I take a sip of my drink, refraining from comment. I should just go. Caleb's got his pick of women, and his sister is pushing single women on him. I'm not part of this equation.

"Who're you here with?" he asks.

I nearly blurt the truth—I came here alone because I couldn't bear one more second of Dad's job-search questions, my two guy friends from high school moved away, and my best friend, Max, is on a date—but it makes me sound pathetic. I'm not pathetic. That's just the way things worked out tonight.

I take another sip of beer, feeling like the odd duck again and too embarrassed about it to move.

He continues. "I remember you played soccer in high school. You were great, zipping in and out, tearing up the field."

My head whips toward his. Am I supposed to believe the golden boy of Summerdale High actually watched girls' soccer and in particular me? Everyone knows Caleb has had a harem of girls trailing him since elementary school.

"Thanks," I say, heat flooding my cheeks despite my vow to remain chill. I don't get a lot of compliments.

His lips curve into a sexy smile that makes my stomach flutter until he asks, "Are you here by yourself?" He glances over my shoulder at an empty barstool. Past that is a group of women I don't know.

I bristle. He must suspect I'm alone and feels sorry for me. Next thing you know, he'll ask me to join in his family's celebration, where I don't belong. I didn't know it would be an engagement party when I got here. I just wanted to get out of the house.

I put some cash on the bar. "I'll let you get back to the festivities." I hop down from the barstool and walk away, feeling his eyes on me.

For a brief moment I consider that he could've been hitting on me. He did ask to buy me a drink. Is it possible he was asking all those questions about who I was with because he hoped I was single? Nah. He's surrounded by curvy women in tight sweaters and slinky dresses over there. And they're not related to him either. The only girl in that family is Sydney.

Even so, I can't resist a glance back over my shoulder. He's already surrounded by smiling beautiful women.

I walk resolutely to the door. He was just talking to me to avoid his matchmaking sister. Obviously he doesn't want to be tied down in a relationship, and I have zero interest in joining his harem. Not that he asked.

2

Two days later, I'm back at my happy place—the smell of grease and rubber, the sound of heavy-duty tools from the next garage bay, the muffled cursing from Dad working nearby. I roll a heavy-duty winter tire into place for an old Toyota, whistling to myself. Give me some tools and an assortment of cars, and I'm like a kid in a candy shop.

After I finish up mounting and balancing the tires, I drive the Toyota out to the nearby lot for customer pickup. I take a look at the work orders on Dad's schedule. We do repairs and light bodywork. Looks like he's already working on the automatic transmission repair. Max is working on a boring oil change on a Honda. Ooh, clutch controllers on a Nissan GT-R. Now that is a sweet ride. I love the complexity of the newer electrical systems. I learned everything I know from Dad. I soaked up his knowledge in the world's best apprenticeship after school, weekends, and every summer. After Mom left when I was twelve, I practically grew up at the shop.

Is it any wonder I'm close with Dad? He was shelter in the storm that followed the end of my modeling career. The day after the photographer declared I was the ugly duckling in reverse, I returned home from school to find my room stripped bare. It might as well have been me stripped bare. There I was, an awkward twelve-year-old, riddled with hormones, vulnerable, still stinging from being dismissed as unattractive by the industry that had previously raved over me, gaping at emptiness.

I stood in my doorway in shock. The closet doors left open to reveal empty hangers. Pageant dresses gone. Every audition outfit gone—soft sweaters, flowing blouses, dresses, skirts, shoes of every color. Everything pretty meant for a pretty girl.

The dresser top cleared of makeup and hair accessories.

Every tiara, blue ribbon, and satin sash removed from their place of honor on my shelves.

I opened my dresser drawers to find only my plain T-shirts and jeans meant for school. Plain clothes for a plain girl.

I rushed through the house, looking for Mom, just as she walked in the front door. "Where's all my stuff?"

Her expression was grim. "I donated what I could and threw out the rest. We don't have a use for it anymore."

My throat clogged over a lump of emotion. "You should've asked me."

She shook her head. "Time to face reality, Sloane. You don't have *it* anymore. Don't be selfish. Maybe another deserving girl could use that stuff."

Hot tears leaked out of my eyes. I didn't deserve nice things.

She sighed. "Tears won't change anything. Now go do your homework."

I ran from the house and straight to Dad at work across town. Mom left shortly after that, and I knew exactly why. The pageants, my modeling career, all that time spent shopping and primping, that was our thing. She'd been my manager, the driving force behind me being a child model and getting so much work from the ages of six to eleven. As soon as I lost my cute kid face, my career ended and so did our bond. She was so disappointed in me, she crossed an ocean and moved to London. She said I was the only reason she'd stayed with Dad as long as she had. After that I only saw her at her annual summer visit. Once she realized I wanted to be a mechanic like Dad, that was the final straw.

The phone calls and emails became less frequent, her obligatory summer visits shorter.

Now I want less to do with her than she does with me. Bond permanently severed.

"Hey, Sloane," a masculine voice calls, interrupting the memories I can never seem to shake loose.

I turn and freeze. *What's Caleb doing here?*

He's at the entrance of an empty bay. This time he's sporting a lumberjack look straight from an outdoor adventure company. Red and black plaid flannel jacket open to a gray turtleneck with dark jeans and hiking boots. I wonder if he takes home complete looks from his modeling gigs. Two days ago, he worked a biker look. I have to admit, lumberjack looks good on him too.

He steps inside the bay.

I suddenly don't know what to do with my hands, so I shove them into the pockets of my blue coveralls. I have the urge to check a mirror in case there's grease smudged on my face, but I resist. I'm at work, and this is how I look at work. My hair's tied back in a low ponytail, no makeup, coveralls, and black steel-toed work boots.

He stops right in front of me, a hint of a smile playing around his lips. Up close, his hazel eyes are green with gold flecks framed by thick lashes. I missed that in the dim light of the bar. I can see why the camera loves him. "Hi, Sloane." His voice is velvet, warm and soft, wrapping around me.

"Hi," I say softly. My pulse kicks up, nerves skittering through me. I thought about our Saturday night chat more than I'd like, trying to figure out if I screwed up. He offered to buy me a drink, and I basically walked away. Does it mean something significant that he showed up here, or does he need a car repair? My judgment may be impaired by the sudden jump in my pulse, my tingling nerves, and every previous misstep I've ever made in the dating world.

"You're here," I say, stating the obvious in hopes he'll tell me why.

His gaze smolders into mine, and my breath catches. A crackling tension fills the air between us. "So I am."

The sound of an air wrench brings me back to reality. I'm at work. Dad and Max are nearby.

I work for a professional tone. "So, uh, how can I help you?"

He gestures to his silver Fiat 124 Spider. "I need my car inspected."

I work hard to hide my disappointment. He's not here for me. He takes good care of his car, a two-seater convertible. It's pristine, which isn't easy with all the rock salt and snow on the road in late November in this part of New York. My own car is less fun. I drive a Subaru Impreza with manual transmission because when your job is to fix cars, you want a break on your own car. My car will go the long haul. I do appreciate a fun ride though.

"Sure, let me see when we have available," I say.

Lowering expectations now.

I move to the short counter with the laptop that has our appointment system. Max raises his brows as I pass by him, giving me a knowing look. My cheeks heat. I filled him in earlier on Saturday night. I've known Max forever. He's three years older than me and started working here part-time when he was in high school. He's only here in the winter now, picking up shifts when his landscaping business is slow. He's also handsome—tousled brown hair, blue eyes, full beard. Truth? Back in my teen years, I had a monster crush on him. I know him too well as a friend now to dwell on silly unrequited crushes. Anyway, Max thought it was funny that I didn't let Caleb buy me a drink.

Well, this worked out fine. Caleb's not into relationships— he said before he had no experience with them—and he also said that women chase him constantly. I want a relationship. So what if he makes my pulse race and my mouth go dry every time I look at him?

Caleb joins me, watching as I click over to the appointment schedule. "So what made you move back to Summerdale? I thought you were a math teacher up in Hartford." That's in Connecticut, a little more than an hour's drive from here.

I give him a sideways glance, surprised he knows that much about me. Maybe Dad blabs to the customers. "I decided teaching isn't for me. I'm working here while I look for another kind of job. Something where I can use my math degree." I hate lying like this, but Dad's close enough to overhear, so I can't admit I haven't done a thing to find a new job. Everything I want is right here.

Caleb leans close, his voice warm and approving. "Well, you look like you're in your natural element."

I feel seen, like he gets that this is where I belong. So few people get that. "I love—"

"She's not staying!" Dad puts in before lumbering to the back of the shop for a tool. Dad's in his fifties, a big teddy bear of a man with the soft belly to match. I take after Mom's petite size, though the rest of me seems to take after his side.

Caleb whispers in my ear, sending a shiver through me. "Sounds like you're getting fired soon. Better get on the job search."

"He just wants me to use my degree," I whisper and then face front, suddenly aware of how close we're standing. He smells woodsy and something distinctly him. My body flushes with heat, both lust and embarrassment. I probably smell like motor oil.

I quickly tap through the schedule. "How's Saturday morning?"

"Actually, I work Saturday mornings at my brother's dojo. You remember Drew? He runs Robinson Martial Arts Academy."

I'm intensely aware of him standing so close to me. Close enough that if I turned and shifted ever so slightly, I'd be in his arms. What would that feel like to have those strong arms around me, to press against the hard planes of his body, to breathe in his woodsy scent?

I shift to face him without any thought beyond needing to explore this delicious feeling. I meet his hazel eyes, and my breath hitches. Then I remember to keep up my part of the conversation. "Sure, I know Drew. I didn't know you worked there too."

His gaze trails from my eyes to my cheeks to my jaw, finally landing on my lips. His voice is gravelly. "Yeah, part time between modeling gigs. Saturday mornings are jam-packed with kids' classes."

I lick my lips, feeling suddenly wobbly. Something's here. An electric attraction. "So you're an instructor?"

"Sure am. I'm a blackbelt." He gives me a once-over from the top of my head to my toes. "We offer beginner adult classes. You should stop by on Wednesday night. First lesson is free."

My stomach drops. *Dammit.* I misread things. He's just drumming up business for his brother's karate school. I must've been imagining his part in this because I wanted him to feel what I feel—blown away. He probably checks out all women the way he checked me out. Just one of those guy things, routinely taking a visual catalog. I glance around the shop, wondering if anyone noticed our little chat. Dad steps through to the restroom in back. Max mouths *hi-ya!* and does a little karate chop. I turn back to Caleb, whose eyes narrow at Max. Guess he saw that.

"Uh, no, thanks," I say. "I'm not into martial arts. How's Thursday at one for inspection?"

"Sure, Thursday works. It's always good to learn self-defense, especially for someone your size."

I give him serious side-eye. I'm well aware I'm five feet one with small muscles, but he didn't have to bring it up. I fill out an appointment card and hand it to him. "There you go."

"Thanks. So who do you hang with locally?"

I look up at him. *Weird question.* Guess he figured out I was alone on Saturday night since I left without telling anyone goodbye. "I'm usually with Max, but he was busy last Saturday. That's why I was solo at the bar." I hitch a thumb toward Max, but he's hidden under a Honda now.

"You only spend time with Max?"

"Yeah. My two friends from high school moved away." Unfortunately, my work friends fell out of touch after I quit. I get it. No one wants to commute an hour plus to get together on the regular.

"Is Max your boyfriend?" Caleb asks.

I snort-laugh. "No. We're friends."

He tilts his head. "Any women friends?"

My back gets up. When I was a kid, girls took my natural reserve to mean I was stuck-up about my modeling career, and they shunned me. When modeling ended, I was so hopelessly out of touch with girl speak, I couldn't manage to get an in. Guys were my friends by default.

I cross my arms. "I see people all the time."

"What do you do with these people you see all the time?" he asks gamely.

I throw my hands up. "Stuff. I don't know."

"How about we get a drink at The Horseman Inn on Thursday night, and I'll introduce you to my sister and her friends. They're always there on ladies' night."

I stare at him, puzzled. *Is he asking me out or offering to help me get women friends?* His sister and her friends have been a tight group since elementary school. They were ahead of me in school, so I don't know them well. Anyway, I've come to terms with the fact that I have nothing in common with other women. They never want to talk cars, racing games, or horror movies. That's what Max and I have in common. It works.

Wait a minute. All this confusion with Caleb finally makes sense. Max must be playing a prank on me. Of course!

I shake my head, smiling. "Did Max put you up to this?"

～

Caleb

I look into her amber eyes, and a jolt zings through me just like on Saturday night, making my pulse thrum through my veins, all of me awake and alive. I had to see her again to find out if my crazy thoughts from the other night were legit. I've never felt this jolt with any other woman. The thoughts bouncing around my head on what that jolt means are so out there, I can't admit them to her or anyone. Bad enough people don't take me seriously because I'm a model. I don't plan on being a model forever, but it pays well, and I save every penny. I have a degree in exercise science, which I plan to use one day, maybe becoming a personal trainer. Something that could help people. I'm more than just a handsome face and muscular bod. Ha!

I gaze down at Sloane, sorely tempted to rub the smudge of grease from her soft-looking cheek. Her creamy skin has a rosy tinge that gives her a healthy glow, her nose is narrow with a small turnup at the end, and her eyes—a golden amber—are a stunning contrast to her dark hair. She's effortlessly beautiful, no makeup or tricks to boost her looks. I'm tired of women who wear tons of makeup, like they're hiding behind a mask. Most women I meet are in the industry. They come on sweet and flirty, but they don't really care about me. They want an introduction to my agent or a certain photographer, or just to raise their status by being seen with me at the right parties. Fakers and wannabes.

Then there was Melissa, a photographer's assistant. I thought she was different. We were hot and heavy for a month until I walked in on her having sex with my roommate in my city apartment. He was the next big "It" model just flown in from Spain. Is it any wonder I've never had a long-term relationship when these are the kind of women I meet?

I want someone confident enough to be themselves.

Someone real with no ulterior motives.

I'm holding out for Ms. Right.

So maybe I have a skewed vision of love because of my parents' legendary courtship (Dad proposed on their first date) and happy marriage. I'm sure they would have had many more years of happiness together if Mom hadn't died too soon.

I remember Sloane from high school and admired her, but I never tried to approach her then because I was a grade younger and a small fry. Embarrassing but true. I was five feet three until I turned sixteen and suddenly shot up, seemingly overnight, to six feet one. I had actual growing pains. Despite always having lots of girl friends, my lack of confidence from being a small fry held me back in the dating game. Dad said I was a late bloomer, but better late than never.

"No, Max didn't put me up to this," I say, amused that Sloane doesn't seem to get that I'm interested in her. "I don't even know Max." I've seen him around but never talked to him. He was four years ahead of me in school.

She plants her hands on her hips and looks over at Max like she's still suspicious he's messing with her. He's too busy lowering a Honda back to the ground to notice her. I have to wonder about them spending all their time together and still being just friends. In my experience, men and women don't last long as friends before one of them admits to lusting for the other. Only natural. I knew my brother Adam didn't have a chance at staying friends with Kayla with all the time they spent together and, sure enough, now they're engaged.

"So how about that drink?" I ask, giving up the pretense of a casual group thing on ladies' night. Though I wouldn't mind introducing her to my sister and her friends. Less competition from Max here.

She turns back to me, her brows furrowing like I'm a puzzle she needs to figure out. "I don't drink."

"I saw you at the bar with a black and tan."

Her rosy cheeks turn bright red, and she mutters something unintelligible.

I duck my head to meet her eyes directly. "Can I at least get your number?"

Her sweet heart-shaped lips purse together. Her delicate features make me want to cradle that face and kiss it all over. Slow kisses to absorb the feel of her. I've never been so close to her before last Saturday when she informed me I gave my dog, Huckleberry, a goofy name. I feel bewitched. I never chase, yet here I am.

"Why?" Sloane asks, her eyes wide.

Why do I want her number? My lips twitch. "So we can hang out some time."

She ducks her head. "Stop messing with me."

"I'm not."

She gives me a wary look, a hint of vulnerability lurking

in her eyes that makes me want to pull her close and protect her from the world. I don't even care that she's in coveralls because it just makes me want to peel them off and see all that creamy skin. I got a glimpse of her petite body last Saturday night in her snug long-sleeved shirt and black yoga pants.

I don't know how to convince her of my sincerity. I barely know her, yet this gut-deep feeling tells me I *need* to know her. She could be my destiny. That's crazy, right? Just because her eyes give me a jolt every time I look into them. Why can't I walk away?

She takes a step back.

"Your eyes are striking," I blurt.

Her eyes flash.

Jolt. My heart thumps harder.

"Pretty lies," she says flatly.

"And I find you intriguing."

Her brows shoot up. "Why?"

"You know more about cars than I do. I only know how to operate one and fill the gas tank."

She holds up a palm, her expression tight. "Just stop. Your obvious charms don't work on me. I'm not your usual kind of woman. I won't be falling at your feet."

The first hint of desperation creeps in. I found my destiny, and she wants nothing to do with me. Cruel fate. I really am crazy, going all Shakespeare over here just because of a jolt. I blame Dad's family legend over his own jolt when he met Mom. I always thought he was exaggerating. He said it meant Mom was the One, which is why he proposed on their first date. It can't be real, right? I need to spend time with Sloane to know for sure.

"I don't expect you to fall at my feet," I say as humbly as I can, even though most women do. I never have to work this hard for a woman.

Her lips part in surprise. "Oh."

I can't resist. I reach out and rub the smudge of grease from her cheek with my thumb. Her skin is just as soft as it looks.

"You had a smudge," I murmur.

She holds a hand to her cheek, staring at me in stunned silence. Her face registers confusion, shock, and something I'm hopeful is interest.

Welp, I'm in this far.

"One drink," I say.

She nods.

I feel someone staring, and turn, catching Max's eye. She needs women friends, like right away.

I turn back to her. "I'll pick you up Thursday at seven." Ladies' night will work. I'll introduce her to Sydney and her friends, get Sloane a drink, and then take her aside for some one-on-one time at a quiet table for dinner.

"I'll meet you there," she says.

She's cautious. That's okay. She doesn't know me that well yet. I hand her my phone. "Put your number in."

She does, her finger jabbing the phone rapidly. She hands it back, not quite meeting my eyes.

"See ya then." I turn and walk out, knowing when to make an exit.

Halfway to my car, something makes me look back. She's got both palms on the counter, head bowed, breathing deeply with her eyes closed.

Excellent. That right there is the dazed effect I'm used to having on women. Glad it's not just me, though it took her longer than I expected to catch up.

Max joins her, giving her ponytail a tug. "Ladies' night sounds fun. Maybe I'll go with you."

She recovers herself, straightening, her eyes lighting up. "Would you?"

I stride back to my car. This guy is a problem.

3

———

Sloane

"No surprise here," I tell Max, feeling strangely deflated. I hold up my phone to show him the text from Caleb. We just closed up shop. Tonight was supposed to be the night I met Caleb for a drink. My gut had been alternately churning and fluttering all day over it. Even knowing Max would be there for support did nothing to calm me. I just wanted it too much, while at the same time I felt I was out of my league with him. I even considered cancelling, but didn't want to be a coward. And now this.

Max reads the text. "Sounds like he's big time."

I look at the text again, trying to think up the perfect casual response. Caleb cancelled on me for a last minute modeling gig in LA. He said it was his first big-brand campaign, but he couldn't share which one yet. He's packing and leaving for the airport shortly. I *knew* he'd cancel. I suspected as much when his inspection appointment was cancelled right before he was supposed to show. My gut feels like a lead weight now. Why should I feel so bad? I half expected it not to work out.

I head for my car at the far end of the lot, and my phone chimes with another text. I stop to read it, my jaw dropping.

Caleb: *Just had an idea. Come with me. The shoot's on Friday, and my flight back isn't until Sunday. Sunny LA for a break from the cold. I'll cover your ticket.*

My pulse accelerates. *Ridiculous.* I can't believe he said that. From one drink to a weekend getaway? An icy wind picks up, and I hurry to my car. Sunny LA does sound tempting.

"We still on for drinks?" Max asks, peering at me over the bed of his white Bellamy Landscapes pickup truck. "I haven't been to ladies' night. I was hoping you'd be my wingman."

"Sure," I say absently, opening the door to my car. I get inside, shut the door, and type a text back to Caleb.

Me: *We barely know each other, and you want me to spend the weekend with you?*

Caleb: *Just thought it would be fun. I'd ask for a room with two beds. No pressure.*

I stare at my phone. This is too weird.

Me: *I don't think so.*

Caleb: *Okay, I'll catch up with you when I get back for that drink.*

Right. I'm sure after an extended stay in LA frolicking with beautiful models, he'll forget all about me. I start the car and head for home. Dad went off on an errand, so I'll have the house to myself to get ready for ladies' night. I'm not especially looking forward to being Max's wingman—he'll probably ditch me as soon as he meets a beautiful woman—but at least the drinks are half price.

Once I get home, I shower and change into a lavender cotton shirt with black leggings and sneakers, leaving my hair down. All the angsty anticipation over tonight is gone. I don't have to attempt makeup, which I'm not great at anyway (Mom's the one who used to doll me up), and I can just be comfortable in my regular clothes. On the rare occasion when I need to look nice for something, I have a simple dressy outfit I change with the seasons—black pencil skirt with cream blouse or cream sweater. I was going to wear the sweater tonight since it's cold. My mind flashes to sunny LA, imagining wearing the light blouse and skirt at some fancy place for dinner with Caleb.

I shake my head at my silly fantasies and grab my small purse. This is better. I didn't feel like shaving my legs anyway.

$\approx$

I step into The Horseman Inn and make my way to the back-room bar. It's noisy, the sound of female laughter carrying. I've never been here on a Thursday night. I didn't even know they had ladies' night with half-price drinks. I hope it's not a major pickup scene. I just want to have a drink, hang with Max for a bit, and go home.

I stop short. The bar is packed with women, only a few guys near the far end of the bar watching the game on the TV and sneaking glances at the women. Crap. Max isn't here yet. There's only one empty seat, and it's near those guys. I guess I could hold the seat, and Max could stand near me.

A high-pitched laugh has my shoulders hitching to my ears. I spent most of high school ignoring the girly whispers and high-pitched giggles behind my back. Let's just say I went through a dark phase, where I dressed all in black in my attempt to fly below the radar. It worked about as well as wearing a bumblebee costume to school, making me stand out when all I wanted to do was disappear. I couldn't wait to graduate and go to our big state university, where it was easy to get lost in the crowd.

"Sloane!" a warm voice exclaims, startling me.

I meet the eyes of a smiling Jenna Larsen. She's a tall thin blonde, who paradoxically owns Summerdale Sweets, the local bakery. You'd think she'd be round from all her good baking. I fixed her Honda Accord recently after a fender bender, and she was very happy with the results.

"Hi, Jenna, how's the Honda running?" I nearly cringe because it sounds like I'm trying to drum up business. Her car was running fine. I fixed the bumper.

"My car's great." She gestures me over. "Come join us. I haven't seen you at ladies' night before."

She's sitting with a group of women not far from the guys

at the end of the bar. The women are all smiling at me. I recognize Sydney Robinson with her long auburn hair. She's Caleb's older sister, the owner of this place. Next to her is Audrey Fox, a petite brunette and our local librarian. There's also a woman with shoulder-length brown hair, big brown eyes, and a doll-like pink mouth. Don't know her.

I walk closer to Jenna, unsure if I should give up the one open seat that I planned to hold while I waited for Max. It's on the opposite side of her group of friends. "I'm supposed to be meeting someone here."

"Well, come over, and when they get here, tell them to join us," Jenna says. "You want a margarita? We got a pitcher." She turns to her friends. "Sloane is an expert mechanic. You should see the magic she did restoring my car and Eli's precious Mustang."

"That was totally your fault," Audrey says. "You rammed into his brand-new Mustang just to get with him."

"Lies!" Jenna declares, her eyes dancing with amusement.

I smile a little. Guess it worked out since they're engaged now.

"He would've cried if he wasn't such a manly man," Sydney puts in.

I feel like I'm intruding on a well-established group, but I make my way over to Jenna anyway. I send a quick text to let Max know I'm with Jenna so he can find me. He might not see me standing next to tall Jenna.

Jenna stands and offers me her barstool.

"That's okay," I say. "I don't want to take your seat."

"Take it, girl. You're the rock star here. My car looks brand new."

I can't take her place with her friends. I don't belong in this group. "I was just doing my job."

She gives me a not-so-gentle nudge forward, so I obligingly take her seat. Then she asks the two older women on the other side of me if they'd mind scooting their barstools a smidge. They do, and Jenna joins me, standing by my side.

"Margarita?" Audrey asks from my other side.

"Sure, thanks."

She signals to the bartender, Betsy, and I'm set up with a glass right away. Audrey pours a huge amount. I'm about to take a sip when I realize Audrey's holding her glass up to me in a toast.

"Oh, sorry." I copy her. Sydney, Jenna, and the brunette I don't know all lift their glasses.

The brunette smiles winningly. "I'm Kayla. Nice to meet you. I'm engaged to Sydney's brother Adam."

I know Adam from around town. He's a master carpenter. "Congrats. Adam does great work."

She beams. "Thanks, he's a true craftsman."

"Enough about your dreamy fiancé," Sydney puts in, rolling her eyes and then grinning. "Welcome, Sloane, to the Thursday Night Wine Club. We always toast when we get our drinks, and since you just got yours, cheers." She reaches past Audrey to clink her glass with mine and then her friends'. We all clink glasses. It takes a while to get to everyone, and the whole time I'm thinking, *Why are we drinking margaritas at wine club?*

Finally, the glass clinking finishes, and I take a sip of my drink.

Audrey leans close. "It was supposed to be Thursday Night Book Club, but no one ever read the book, and everyone drank wine, so Sydney renamed it."

"Ah. Why're we drinking margaritas instead of wine?" I ask.

"Jenna requested it because she just got engaged. She felt it was more celebratory."

Jenna shoves her hand in front of my face, wiggling her fingers to show off a sparkly diamond ring.

"Congrats," I say. "So two of you ladies are engaged to Robinsons."

"Yup," Jenna says. "Audrey's still single."

Audrey nods once. "I'm waiting for Mr. Right."

"Gonna be waiting a long time since Mr. Right doesn't exist," Sydney says.

"You should try eLoveMatch again," Kayla says.

Audrey sighs and turns to me. "Have you done the online

dating thing?"

I sit up straighter, surprised she asked me. I was just sort of listening here on the periphery of the female group like usual. "Me? No."

"Are you single?" Kayla asks.

"Yes," I say.

Audrey slices a hand through the air. "Well, it's rough out there in the online dating world. People finesse their photos and flat-out lie on their profiles. It's a real grab bag of nasty surprises."

"I can imagine," I say.

She offers me a fist bump. "Solidarity, sister."

I fist-bump her, still a little surprised to be included.

"Ooh," Kayla says. "Sloane must know lots of single guys from work. Not to mention all the guys who come in fussing over their cars. Do you have someone you could introduce to Audrey? She's looking for a guy who's a reader."

"That's on my short list," Audrey replies. "I'd also like him to have good manners."

"A perfectly reasonable short list," Kayla assures her.

I lift my brows. "Wouldn't you be more likely to meet a guy who likes books at the library than at my dad's garage? I wouldn't know about their manners just from a guy dropping off their car either."

Audrey tosses back the rest of her margarita and wipes her mouth with the back of her hand. "You'd think the library would be filled with single guy readers, wouldn't you? Makes total sense, but no! Not a single one! Unless I'd like a single guy past *seventy*. Well, then, there's three of those." She holds up three fingers. "Ooh, the choices!"

"Uh…" I sip my margarita, unsure what to say.

"Aud, you're getting loud over here, bitching about guys," Jenna says from just over my shoulder. "I think you've reached your limit of margaritas."

"This is only my second one!" Audrey protests.

Jenna squeezes Audrey's shoulder. "And you're five feet one, one hundred pounds soaking wet. You can't keep up."

"So am I," I tell Audrey. "Though I can go as far as three beers." That's my usual drink.

Audrey giggles. "Sure, let's go with that weight." Then she whispers in my ear, "I haven't seen that number on the scale since I was thirteen."

"Wow, I feel so tall suddenly," Kayla says. "I'm two inches taller than you two."

"You're a real green bean," Jenna says.

I burst out laughing. I don't know why. Maybe because Kayla looks nothing like a green bean. She's got a compact curvy body, and her cheeks are round.

"Looks like someone's having a good time," Max says from behind me, giving my hair a tug.

I turn, smiling. "Hey, you found me. Look at you, dressed so nice, and you trimmed your beard too. You almost look civilized." Instead of his usual T-shirt and jeans, he put on a light blue button-down shirt and dark jeans with no holes in them. He's wearing leather shoes instead of sneakers too. This must be his pick-up-women outfit. I'm never with him when he does that. That's when I remember my part—wingman for Max.

"I think you probably know everyone, but just in case, this is Jenna, Audrey, Kayla, and Sydney."

Max points to each of them in turn. "Jenna, Audrey, Sydney, missing Harper." He turns to me. "They were in my grade in school." He gives Kayla a charming smile. "You must be the new Harper."

Kayla lifts one shoulder. "I'm just me. Harper's on another plane, a superstar." Harper's a famous actress now.

"You could shine up there too," Max says, a hint of flirtation in his voice.

Audrey swivels in her seat. "Save it, Max. Kayla's engaged."

Kayla holds up her hand, showing off her ring, but Max only has eyes for Audrey. He gets serious, his voice taking on a soft tone I've never heard from him before. "How've you been, Aud?"

"Fine," Audrey says primly. "How're you?"

"Good," he says.

"She's single," Kayla puts in.

Audrey sends her a murderous glare.

It occurs to me that Max and Audrey have a history. I didn't know. Max and I weren't close when we were teens. I mostly admired him from across the garage bay. We started hanging out when I was on break from college.

Kayla shakes her head. "Never mind. She's looking for Mr. Right, and I'm guessing you're not him? No offense."

"Can I sit here?" Max asks me, gesturing for my seat next to Audrey.

"Sure."

Audrey grabs my arm, holding me in place. "Stay. Max, you should know that my biological clock is ticking. I'm looking for a husband and kids, preferably in that order, as soon as possible."

Max goes ramrod straight, which is odd because he's usually so laid-back. "Geez, you really know how to scare the crap out of a guy."

"Thank you. It's how I separate the Mr. Rights from the completely Mr. Wrongs."

Max's voice turns harsh. "So I'm Mr. Wrong? I did the right thing, and you know it. You think I wanted—"

"Just go away!" Audrey exclaims, her cheeks flushing red with anger.

My eyes widen, and then my jaw gapes as a large guy approaches with a lethal look in his eyes. He's got longish dark hair and moves like a sleek jaguar. "Is there a problem here?" he growls.

"Drew," Audrey says in a breathy voice. "No, it's fine. Don't worry about it."

Oh shit. I didn't recognize him at first—Caleb's older brother Drew. He used to have a crew cut with a clean-shaven jaw. Now his hair is longer, and his jaw is heavily stubbled. Former Army Ranger, current owner of Robinson Martial Arts Academy. Not a man to be messed with. I shoot a panicked look at Max, but he already knows the danger level here.

Max holds his palms up. "Just talking here, man, catching up."

"She asked you to go," Drew says through his teeth.

Max takes a step back. "No problem. Come on, Sloane."

Is it bad that I want to keep hanging with these women? I've never been in the thick of conversation like this before. But then I remember Max came here tonight in support of me, knowing I was nervous about meeting Caleb for a drink, and when that didn't work out, I agreed to be his wingman. A wingman wouldn't ditch their best friend.

"Bye, ladies, thanks for the drink," I say, tossing some cash on the bar.

Jenna grabs my arm. "Wait. Give me your number. We need more warm bodies to help with Winterfest. Wednesday night meetings. Are you free then?"

"You want me?" I blurt.

"Absolutely. These ladies are doing their part already. Peer pressure, come on!"

"One of us, one of us," Kayla chants.

"Okay, okay," I say with a laugh. I give her my number and say bye to everyone.

I join Max waiting a distance away. "What's the deal with you and Audrey?"

"Ancient history," he says, striding ahead of me toward the front dining room.

I hurry to catch up with him. His legs are much longer. He pushes through the front door, and I follow in his wake. He pushed the door so forcefully there's time for both of us to go through.

"You never mentioned her," I say once we get outside.

He scrubs a hand over his face. "We went out senior year and broke up. Now you know." He sounds upset, even though it was more than ten years ago.

"Sorry. Is this the first time you've talked to her?"

"More than a quick hello, yes." He looks over my shoulder back at The Horseman Inn. "It's fine. Like I said, ancient history." He focuses back on me. "You want to come over and play *Blazer*?" That's our favorite racing game.

"Sure. Think you'll ever go to ladies' night again? There were other single women there."

He grimaces. "You couldn't pay me to go."

I panic for a moment that if Caleb asks me for a drink next ladies' night, Max won't be there for backup, but then I realize that's not even a real concern. Caleb is probably flirting with the flight attendant and sipping champagne in first class at this very moment. Once he lands in California, he'll be surrounded by beautiful models all weekend long. That's his world, and I don't belong in it.

I get in my car and pull my phone out of my purse. I never did give Caleb an answer about meeting up a different time. I almost feel like I should thank him for mentioning ladies' night because I had a nice time. Oh, there's another text from him.

Caleb: *Sorry to miss tonight. I was looking forward to it. I don't usually travel that much. Most of my gigs are in NYC.*

My hand goes to my pounding heart. He sounds so sincere.

Am I really going to do this? He's part of a world I was rejected from with traumatic results.

I scrunch my eyes shut tight, thinking hard. It's not Caleb's fault I have this baggage. It's one drink. I don't have to be part of his modeling world. We'll be safely here in Summerdale, where I'm comfortable. Okay, I'm doing this. Now to think of the perfect flirty reply.

Max honks his horn at me before peeling out of the lot. I toss my phone back in my purse. Better not to attempt to flirt. It'll come out all wrong. And you can't take back a text.

4

Caleb

I texted Sloane a few times over the weekend, giving her updates on my work and the sights I was seeing. I had a great time working with the people at Cali Pop, a major chain of clothing stores. Sloane only sent back short one-word replies: *Cool. Nice. Okay.* Now I'm back home in Summerdale, unsure what my next move is with her. Is that her texting style, or is she not interested in meeting up? She never did agree to rescheduling our drink date. It's Monday now. I really don't want to show up at her work again with her dad and Max as witnesses.

Screw it. I'll just call her. It goes to voicemail. I look up the garage's number and try there.

"Murray's," a gruff voice answers, probably her dad. Max sounds smooth, like he's working hard to be charming.

"Hi, Mr. Murray?"

"Speaking."

"It's Caleb Robinson. Is Sloane available?"

The phone clatters. "Sloane! Phone for you."

A few moments later, she picks up. "Hello?"

"Hi, it's Caleb."

"Oh, hi."

She sounds a little surprised I called. Did she think I

ditched her and wouldn't follow up? "I'm calling to reschedule that drink. You want to try this Thursday? I can introduce you to Sydney and friends, and maybe you guys will hit it off." Sloane's younger than them, so I figure she doesn't know them well.

Silence.

"Or dinner," I say, feeling a little desperate. "How about tomorrow at The Horseman Inn? They have a new chef, and it's actually really healthy farm-to-table food. If you're into that. I pay attention to nutrition, exercise, healthy lifestyle, all that stuff." I close my eyes. *Shut up.* I'm babbling because for the first time in a long time, I'm unsure of where I stand with a woman.

"Okay."

"Okay?" I echo way too loudly. "Okay. Great."

"A drink would be better."

"Oh." She doesn't want to commit to spending too much time with me, keeping it casual. Just because I felt a jolt when her amber eyes met mine doesn't mean she felt the same. "Sure, a drink. That's fine."

"I'll meet you there tomorrow. Hold on." The phone clatters down.

I wait for several long minutes. I must've interrupted her in the middle of some crucial car repair. Finally, she comes back. "How's seven?"

"That works. Sorry for interrupting. I'm sure you're really busy."

"Actually, I was on break."

"Ah." Then why did I have to wait so long for her to tell me the time? Oh no. She's not bringing Max along, is she? He was supposed to join us last Thursday. I can't ask because then it sounds like I'm jealous of Max, which I am. I'm sure he's just biding his time before making his move on Sloane. I'll just have to win her over before he can. "Okay, see you then. Looking forward to it."

"Mmm-kay, bye."

I hang up, my brows scrunching in deep thought. Not for the first time I wish Dad were still around to talk to. He died two years ago from an advanced cancer they discovered too late. A great man I still consider my hero. He really stepped up after Mom died when I was eight. One day I hope to be just like him with a family of my own. *Whoa.* That's the first time I considered having a family, which means marriage. Must be something in the water around here. My older brothers Adam and Eli are both engaged. My older sister, Sydney, is happily married. Just me, the youngest, and Drew, the oldest, are still living the bachelor life.

Ah, hell, who am I kidding? I'm happy for my siblings, but deep down I know that's not what got me thinking along these lines. It was that jolt I felt with Sloane. *Dad, see what you put in my head with your mushy stories about Mom?*

I exhale sharply, anticipation making my stomach jumpy. I wonder what Sloane would think about that settling-down part.

～

Sloane

"Where are you two off to tonight?" Dad asks in a jovial tone, looking from me to Max. We just finished up work and are on our way out together because I want to be sure Max will be on time for the bar tonight.

"Be there in a sec," I tell Dad over my shoulder.

Dad waves in acknowledgment as he walks to his small office to the left of the front door of the shop.

I continue walking out with Max to the parking lot. I'll explain to Dad in a minute. I don't want him to get the wrong idea about me and Max. That could get embarrassing at work. Dad's not subtle at all.

"I still don't get why you need me," Max says to me in a low voice.

"You were fine coming along on ladies' night before."

"Yeah, and this isn't ladies' night. What if Caleb wants to make a move on you? No guy appreciates a cockblock."

"That's not happening," I sputter, shocked he'd say that. "We're in public at a bar. It's fine if you're there. Max, you promised." I need an objective opinion on Caleb. Is he sincerely interested in me? I can't help but think he's only chasing me because I didn't immediately fall into his lap like most women do. Guys love a challenge.

"Fine." Max shakes his head and walks to his truck.

I meet up with Dad. He's sitting in his cushioned swivel chair behind a beat-up black metal desk. He has his glasses on with the laptop open in front of him, which makes me think he's staying late to do the books.

I take the black plastic chair across from him. "I can do that for you. I'll set up a spreadsheet that'll pull stuff automatically and spit out the totals nice and neat."

He lowers his glasses to look at me. "And then when you leave, I'm stuck with a spreadsheet full of formulas that make no sense to me. No, thanks."

I press my lips together, guilt weighing heavily on me. I've been home five months now. He bought the excuse that school districts aren't hiring for next year yet. That would be the easy next move, starting over at another teaching job closer to home, but that's not what I want.

"Dad, I'd really like to stay on here and help you. Once it's spring, you'll lose Max. I can help you pick up the slack." Max is only part-time seasonally when his landscaping business is slow.

"You didn't graduate college with honors to work here." He leans forward and taps his forehead. "You've got a brain. Use it."

"So do you." I know I took after him. We think the same way, both of us analytical problem solvers.

He sets his glasses on the desk and closes the laptop. "And I didn't get the opportunity for college. Your grandfather died suddenly of a heart attack when I was seventeen. I had to take over here or my younger siblings wouldn't have had food on the table. I want better for you, and that's that." Dad dropped out of high school and later took the GED test for the diploma.

We've had this conversation before, circling the same reasons why he wants a different life for me.

I lean forward. "But you didn't have a choice. I'm choosing this if you'll let me."

"Not happening, Sloane. End of discussion."

I exhale sharply and slump back in my seat. I don't know how to make him see this is the right choice for me. It's not throwing away my education. I'm grateful for it, and I know I can always go back to teaching if I have to, but I want a different life for myself. I suppose I could get a mechanic job at another garage. The idea doesn't appeal. I like living in Summerdale, and I love working with Dad. He really is the best mechanic.

He brightens. "Now, what's going on with you and Max? I saw you two in a very animated conversation earlier. Has he finally asked you out?"

I jolt upright, my cheeks flaming. "*Da-a-ad.* That's ridiculous. We're friends."

He gives me a knowing look. "I remember how you used to follow him around like a puppy dog when you were younger." He dances his fingers across the desktop.

"Stop. We're just going for a drink tonight. It's a group thing."

"What group?"

"Just some locals Max knows. It's no big deal." I don't want to bring up Caleb in case it goes nowhere. Also, the fact that he's part of the modeling world is a big red flag for me.

He eyes me. "Okay, have fun. For the record, I think Max is a good guy."

I stand. "Of course he is. I wouldn't be friends with a jerk. See ya tomorrow."

I walk to my car, the cool breeze feeling good on my overheated face. Max doesn't think of me that way. It was hard to convince him to come with me tonight. I had to promise beers are on me next time we go out.

Two hours later, I'm at the bar waiting on two guys. Well, now, this isn't awkward at all. I made an attempt to look nice, brushing my hair out and putting on mascara and pink lip gloss. That's about as far as my makeup skills go. I'm wearing my cream sweater with jeans and black flats. I never did get the hang of heels, which would've been a great height booster. Ah well. The awkward wobble would've negated any advantage of height.

It's Tuesday night and pretty quiet at The Horseman Inn. I saw Kayla having dinner with her fiancé, Adam, in the front dining room. She gave me a warm hello. The bar only has a couple of guys in their thirties watching the game on the TV. They must be new in town. A lot of new families have moved into town since I left for college. Our regional high school was named one of the best in the state, and Summerdale became more popular with young families.

I wipe my clammy hands on my jeans. I swear if Max doesn't show up tonight, I'll kill him. He knows how much this means to me. I don't want to be a sucker falling for a pretty line from a guy who's way out of my league. I probably wouldn't be so cautious if Caleb weren't a model. He has his pick of beautiful women constantly surrounding him. What would he want with plain old me?

"Can I get you a drink?" Betsy asks. She's a cool bartender, probably late twenties, who started here a few years back. She's an unusual combination of punk with her pink hair and piercings and retro with her outfits. Today she's wearing a blue and white striped shirt over a white skirt with daisies embroidered on it. I wonder if people consider her an odd duck too. Maybe we should hang out. I don't know how to ask, so I just smile.

"I'll wait for my friend before ordering," I say. "Thanks."

"You got it." Her phone rings, and she answers. "Hey, cutie. I heard you're shopping for a new look. You know I'm your girl for all things fashion." She laughs. "I'll officially have my fashion design degree in three more semesters. It counts."

I shift to face the entrance of the room. Fashion design is like the opposite of fixing cars. I don't think we'd have anything to talk about. Max strides in, and I leap off the barstool, meeting him halfway.

I stop in front of him. "You made it before he did. Let's sit at the bar and act casual."

He looks over my head at the bar. "There's only two other people here. This is going to look way too obvious."

"Do you know those guys?"

"One of them is a client."

"So you can sit with them and just casually observe Caleb and later tell me what you think."

He rests a hand on top of my head. He always does that because I'm short. "The things I do for you."

I grin. "What have you done for me? This is the first time I asked you for a favor like this."

"Don't think I didn't notice you grabbing all the plum repair jobs and leaving me with oil changes."

I push his hand off my head. "I have no idea what you're talking about."

We walk over to the bar. I take my seat, and he lingers, standing next to me.

He taps my nose. "Plus every time we have popcorn, you snarf the buttery pieces from the bottom of the bowl before I can get any."

"I make the popcorn, so I get the primo pieces. I do keep your favorite beer in my refrigerator."

He grunts and orders a beer.

"Hey, Sloane," Caleb says, appearing suddenly right in front of me.

Crap! Max is with…oh, not anymore. He drifted over to his client, and they're shaking hands.

"Hi," I say, tucking my hair behind my ears. My hands never know what to do when Caleb's around. Why does he have to look like he just stepped out of a glossy magazine ad? He's wearing a black down jacket with jeans and hiking boots. It's a casual look, but he's so magnetic it's like he lifts the clothes to a new level. No wonder he's a model.

His hazel eyes are intent on mine. "I'm glad you agreed to meet up again."

"Sure, it's not your fault you had to work."

Look at me, pulling off casual! It's almost as if I haven't been sweating it out for the last fifteen minutes in anticipation of this moment.

He takes off his jacket, revealing a white thermal Henley that outlines the swell of his shoulders and biceps. He smells woodsy and clean like he just took a shower. My pulse beats rapidly. I'm hyperaware of him, of me, every nerve ending at attention.

He glances up, his eyes narrowing. I turn to see what has his attention—Max. I consider acting surprised to see Max, but I'm terrible at fake stuff, so I just sit there, hoping Caleb doesn't suspect why Max is here.

Caleb turns to me. "What would you like to drink?"

I relax a little because he didn't mention Max. "The Twisted House ale on tap is good."

He takes the barstool next to mine, sitting at an angle toward me. He signals to Betsy, and she walks over, smiling at him.

"You and Sloane, huh?" she asks.

"We'll see," he says with a charming smile. "It's early yet. This is our first time out."

"Good luck, handsome," she says, pouring the beers.

Obviously she doesn't think he needs luck.

After we get our beers, he shifts, putting his feet on the lower rung of my barstool, one leg between mine, one leg on the outside of mine. He's not touching me but we feel entangled. I flush with heat. It's both intimate and unnerving. There's no way I could make a fast exit.

"So how was your shoot?" I ask.

"Great. There were four of us, two guys, two girls. We did a bunch of photos on the beach and on the Venice boardwalk. Everyone got along well, and the photographer was funny. She made it really relaxed and fun."

"Cool. So can you reveal what it was for?"

He leans close, his voice deep and soft by my ear. "Swear you won't tell a soul?" He pulls back to meet my eyes, so close I can barely breathe. A hint of amusement sparkles in his eyes. "Swear?"

"Yes."

He leans forward to whisper in my ear, "Cali Pop."

"That's big."

He grins. "Yup. And I just found out they're doing a big East Coast campaign. My agent says I'll be plastered on one of those jumbo screens in Times Square." That's a crazy touristy area in New York City filled with giant billboard screens.

"Your head will be huge, like King Kong."

He barks out a laugh. "Never been compared to a giant ape before, but yeah, I'll be bigger than real life, that's for sure."

"I was never a fan of Times Square, but I always liked visiting the city. I went there a lot growing up." My best memories with Mom are lunch and shopping in the city. Dad made it a point to take me there regularly after she left because he knew I missed it.

His hazel eyes sparkle. "Yeah? We should go. What do you like about it?"

I wave a hand around vaguely. "Just the energy, always something going on, people rushing here and there. Window-shopping. And the food. Love the food."

"Yes! So much variety. You can get anything there, any ethnicity, fusions of flavors."

"Even the hole-in-the-wall places can be good."

He points at me. "It's a date. We're hitting the city together."

I bite my lower lip. That sounds promising. He's already thinking of our next date. He takes a sip of beer, so I do the same.

"So do you love being a model?" I ask. It's the one thing about him that makes me wary.

He inclines his head. "Yeah, I'm happy with where I'm at now, but I don't plan on doing this forever. My schedule's all over the place; cash flow is uneven. I can see a time down the road when I'll want a more settled life with a steady paycheck."

He sounds so mature, and somehow that's the biggest turn-on of all. He's twenty-five, but he's not wild and all over the place. He's got his head on straight. "What would you do after you retire from modeling?"

He looks thoughtful. "I don't know. I have a degree in exercise science, but I can't see myself as a gym teacher. Maybe a personal trainer. I have to look into what's involved. For now, I'm going with the flow, especially since I landed that major brand. My agent says after the holidays, I'll probably be flooded with offers for big campaigns."

Maybe he won't be sticking around here after all. At that sobering thought, I focus on my drink, taking a sip. "Cool. Sounds like things are going really well for your career."

"They are, but Summerdale's home. Ultimately."

I paste on a smile. "Sure."

His eyes narrow at a point over my shoulder. "Is there a reason Max keeps looking over here?"

I lift one shoulder, forcing myself not to look. "I'm sure it's accidental. We're just in his line of vision, that's all."

"Did you come here together?"

"No. I was here waiting for you, and then he came in." My face flushes. It's true, but I did ask Max to be here. I grab my beer and chug. Then I search for a napkin. Mine is wet from condensation on the glass. I can't find one, so I discreetly wipe my mouth with my fingers. Aren't I just the picture of femininity? This is why most guys want to be my buddy, not my boyfriend. Unless we hang out a bunch and they get horny or whatever. I'm convenient, not sought after, which is exactly why Max is here to tell me the real deal about Caleb.

"Did you two used to go out?" Caleb asks.

I burst out laughing. "No."

"Why is that funny?"

I calm down, still smiling. "Because we're friends."

"Do you have a lot of guy friends?"

"Yeah, well, not right now, but usually I'm friends with guys. I don't have a lot in common with women."

"Because you're a mechanic?"

I sip my beer, unwilling to share the nitty-gritty. "I don't know. It's just always been that way."

He studies me for a moment, and I try not to fidget. "You probably have something in common with Kayla. That's my brother Adam's fiancée. She's a biostatistician, so you two could talk math stuff."

"I don't usually talk math stuff, but yeah, I guess. I actually met her already last Thursday at ladies' night. Since I'd been planning on coming here for a drink with you, after you cancelled, I showed up. She's very friendly."

"She is. You two should hang out."

I sip more beer. Kayla didn't ask to hang out, and I feel weird asking her to. I mean, I only met her once. I'll see Jenna tomorrow night for a Winterfest meeting, but that's just because she needs more help, nothing personal.

Caleb leans close, his voice husky. "So what're you into besides food tours of the city?"

I smile, though my heart's beating so loudly in my ears I can barely focus. "Cars."

He leans back. "I know very little about cars, but I'm pretty good with them virtually. Love *Blazer*. You know, the racing video game?"

My favorite game!

I grab his arm impulsively and meet the hard muscle of his bicep, the heat of his skin penetrating the shirtsleeve. I stare at my hand on his arm, knowing I should let go but somehow unable to move. "I love that game," I tell his bicep.

"Cool."

I drop my hand from his arm, suddenly embarrassed. "We should play, though I should warn you, I'll probably kick your ass." I give him a sideways glance.

He inclines his head.

Crap. Did I sound like a buddy challenging him to a game? Ugh. Why can't I get this flirting thing right?

I risk a peek back at Max, a silent question in my eyes. *Am I wasting my time here?* Max jerks his chin at me, encouraging me to go back to my conversation.

I turn back to Caleb. "So I guess now you know what I'm into. What're you into?"

His lips curve up. "You."

My mouth flaps, my brain scrambling for an appropriate response. Then I realize it's just a line. "You're good. I'm sure that works for you all the time. You say what're you into, and then the other person asks the same—" I go stock-still at the familiar feeling of a large male hand on top of my head.

"Hey, cupcake," Max says, grinning down at me.

Cupcake?

Max ruffles my hair and looks at Caleb. "Isn't she as cute as a cupcake?"

Caleb's eyes narrow. "Sure."

Obviously he doesn't agree. I smooth my hair down. *God, this is so mortifying. Why did Max ask him that? Go back to your spying from a distance!*

Max has a wicked gleam in his eyes as he reaches over, picks up my beer, and takes a sip. "Pretty good. What is it?"

"Twisted House ale," Caleb bites out.

Max helps himself to another long swallow of my beer. We always sample each other's beers if it looks tasty, but I'm supposed to be on a date here. I think. I'm still not sure what exactly this thing is with Caleb.

I glance at Caleb, whose jaw is tight, a muscle ticking there.

Max sets my glass down on the bar top. "Awesome. Sloane, next time you pick up some beer to keep in your fridge for me, get some of that. I think that's even tastier than my usual."

"Sure," I say. He pays for the pizza; I keep his beer in stock.

Max smirks at Caleb.

Caleb stands abruptly, facing off with Max. Oh crap! I don't want them fighting. Hold up, are two men fighting over me? This is unprecedented! I'm not even sure who would win. Caleb's shoulders are bulkier, but that's from the gym. Max is strong from hard physical labor and street smart. On the other hand, Caleb's a blackbelt. That's probably an advantage.

They stare each other down.

"Guys?" I say uncertainly.

Caleb speaks between his teeth. "Sloane and I are on a date. You need to go."

Max turns to me, resting his hand on top of my head. "Is that what you want, cupcake?"

I shove his hand away. "Stop calling me cupcake! You're embarrassing the shit out of me."

Max cocks his head. "You didn't answer my question. You okay here with him?"

"She's fine," Caleb answers for me in a vaguely threatening tone.

I can't take any more embarrassment. "Yes, I'm okay. Thank you for checking in. Bye, Max."

He gives my shoulder a nudge and strides away, heading toward the exit. Caleb's back is to him, so he doesn't see Max turn around and mouth *he's into you* or the obscene gesture he makes indicating we'll be getting it on soon.

I duck my head, tucking my hair behind my ears. Max was testing Caleb on his way out. I guess he's right because Caleb seemed kind of jealous and really wanted me to himself. Go figure. A gorgeous male model wants me—the buddy to most guys, the odd duck among women.

"What an ass," Caleb mutters.

"He's actually a great guy."

"Right. So great you keep him in beer. Just a minute, I'll be right back."

"Oh, okay." I sip my beer and crane my neck, hoping he's not going after Max. It's pretty quiet, no loud male voices, so I guess Caleb's just using the men's room. I stare at the TV over the bar. Now that I know he's into me, for real, not just as friends or a challenge, what do I do with him?

5

Caleb

I don't care what Sloane says about her and Max just being friends, I can tell Max is into her. And he was letting me know, telling her to keep a certain beer in her fridge for him right in front of me. Not to mention the fact that he's shown up on our dates twice. The first time I had to cancel, but it still counts because he invited himself along.

And why wouldn't he be into Sloane? She's smart, beautiful, down to earth. This is not a flaky woman obsessed with makeup and all that superficial stuff so many of the women I meet are into. Hazard of my job, I guess. I didn't realize how much I wanted to be with the kind of woman I grew up with until I met up again with Sloane. She's a hometown girl who still enjoys the city just like me. I like her quirky, unassuming nature. She's just so genuine. And she knows what she wants in life, even when her career choice goes against the norm. I've never met anyone like her before, and I don't think I ever will. She's unique.

I walk over to the front dining room, where Adam and Kayla are having dinner. I pull out a wooden chair at their round table, shift the chair close to Kayla, and take a seat. Sloane can't see us from the bar area. Kayla smiles at me, her bright brown eyes sparkling.

"Have a seat," Adam says dryly. My brother is six years older than me. We resemble each other except his coloring is darker—dark brown hair, brown eyes, and a scruffy jaw.

"How's it going with Sloane?" Kayla asks.

I lower my voice. "We barely started talking when Max came over, his hands all over her, sharing her drink, and then telling her to keep his new favorite beer in stock for the next time he stops by her place!" I get loud at the end there. I can't help it.

"They're a thing?" Adam asks.

"I saw him at ladies' night last Thursday too," Kayla says. "They—"

"Wait, she came here with him then too?" I *knew* he was here tonight for a reason. She said he arrived after her, so I'm not sure if she invited him or if he showed up to intervene. Either way, he's a major problem.

Adam goes back to eating his roast chicken, letting Kayla fill me in. Max was with Sloane last Thursday night, but had to abruptly leave after he pissed off Audrey. Apparently, Max and Audrey have a history. If they got back together, that would work for me, but that's not why I'm here.

"Can I ask you a favor?" I ask Kayla.

Adam sets his fork down to listen.

"Of course!" Kayla says brightly.

I whisper in her ear, "Could you hang with Sloane? She just moved back to town a few months ago, her high school friends moved away, and I think she could use a friend."

She gives me a knowing look. "You mean someone besides Max."

I incline my head.

"No problem." She quickly fills Adam in, who's still leaning forward, trying to hear. She turns back to me, whispering with enthusiasm, "I like her. I'll just invite her to join us this Thursday for ladies' night too. And I'll be sure to tell her not to bring Max this time. It wouldn't be fair to Audrey."

"Perfect."

Kayla pops out of her seat. "I'll go ask her right now and get her number so we can stay in touch."

As soon as Kayla leaves, Adam raises his brows. "You really feel like you need to keep Sloane away from her only friend just because he's a guy?"

I try to soothe my guilty conscience by reasoning Kayla would be a much better friend to Sloane than Max. Doesn't work. I'm jealous. Not proud of it, but there it is. I've never been jealous in my life.

"Look at you and Kayla," I say defensively. "You swore up and down you were just friends, spent tons of time together, and next thing you know, you're engaged."

Adam smiles. "I'm so damn lucky."

"Yes, yes, we know. Kayla is the best woman to ever walk the earth."

His gaze drifts to where she just left. "She's everything."

"We all love her, no question." I glance nervously over toward the back dining room, belatedly worrying that Kayla might reveal more than I'd like to Sloane. Kayla is an open book, who says whatever she thinks, whenever she thinks it. I'm known for always saying what I think too, but I use discretion. I'm not sure Kayla knows the meaning of the word.

Adam seems to read my mind. "Oh, yeah. Kayla's spilling her guts, telling Sloane you're really into her. You are, aren't you? I haven't seen you so concerned about who a woman spends time with before. Usually you walk away easily, always another woman waiting around the corner."

"There's something different about her." I don't want to admit I felt the jolt Dad always talked about. He called it a thunderbolt. According to family legend, after Dad proposed to Mom on their first date, he had to propose twice more before he got a yes. Took a month from first date to engaged, and they married shortly after that. It didn't happen that way for my siblings. Adam would tease me, and then the rest of my siblings would pile on.

"Different how?"

I lift one shoulder, keeping the intensity of my feelings for her to myself. "She's cool. A little mysterious, like there's a lot she's not saying."

"Maybe she's just shy."

I consider that for the first time. Her short texts, her rosy cheeks, the way she doesn't flirt much or at all. She seemed much more comfortable talking to Max than me. I hadn't even considered that was why I've been so uncertain where I stand with her. I feel so much better if that's all it is.

"How do you get past the shyness?" I ask. Adam has always been reserved, preferring his own company or small groups to a crowd. Some people called him shy growing up, though he speaks up when something matters to him.

"Why're you asking me?"

"Because you're quiet, keep to yourself."

"By choice."

I figure he's not going to be any help, but then he surprises me.

"She just needs time to warm up to you. Be patient."

"Thanks."

Kayla appears, smiling widely.

"Guess it went well," I say under my breath to Adam.

"The woman is a force of nature," he says proudly.

Kayla takes her seat and announces, "Mission accomplished! You know, I didn't realize we were both math majors. She said you mentioned my job to her. It's not often I meet a fellow woman math major. Now that's the start of a beautiful numerical friendship."

"Awesome. I'm going to get back to her." I head toward the bar area.

"Break a leg!" she calls.

For the first time, I actually feel like I might need some luck. Sloane has me off balance.

I find Sloane next to her empty glass of beer and join her. "Would you like another drink?" *Since Max drank half your beer?* I so wanted to smack that smirk off his face.

She's facing the bar, not looking at me. "That's okay."

I sit next to her. "How about dinner? I could get us a table."

"I already ate." Finally, she meets my eyes. "Kayla invited me to ladies' night on Thursday."

"Great. You should go."

She searches my expression. "You didn't tell her to do that, did you?"

I keep a straight face. "Why would you say that?"

"I don't know. You left, she came over, and then you came back after she left. Just seemed a little coincidental."

"I ran into her and told her about you. She liked the fact that you had math in common."

Her eyes narrow. "Truth?"

Crap. I can't lie to her face. "Okay, full confession, I also told her you could use a friend. She was all over that. She's new in town, found a place here, and that makes her want to help other people feel included."

Her cheeks flush red. "But *I'm* not new in town."

"You're kinda new. You just came back a few months ago, and you said your high school friends moved away. Sorry for a little friend matchmaking. I just thought you'd like each other."

She turns back to the bar. "I don't need your help making friends, Caleb. You embarrassed me, telling her to make nice with me. It makes me look pathetic."

My gut clenches. Crap. I played that all wrong. "No, it's not like that at all. Sorry. I got jealous, okay?"

She turns back to me, her eyes wide. "Jealous of what?"

"Max spends so much time with you, it's obvious he's into you, and I wanted you to spend time with someone else." I shove a hand through my short hair. "I'm the pathetic one here."

She stares at me, searching my expression.

"I don't know what's come over me. I just never felt…"

"Felt what?" she asks softly.

The thunderbolt. I can't say it. Family legend looms large in my mind, but it's silly. Love at first sight isn't a real thing. So why do I feel compelled to be with her? Normally I can walk away easily.

"Can we start over?" I search my brain desperately for a change of topic. "Let's play a game called worst thing I ever did. Not counting setting you up on a friend date. I really am sorry about that. I'm usually not the jealous type."

She's quiet for a long moment.

I hold my breath. *Did I screw everything up on our first date?*

Her lips curve up a little. "Okay, you first."

I let out a breath. "Okay, here goes. I mooned the audience at my first-grade play."

She slaps a hand over her mouth. "Serious?"

"Yup, the play was so boring I had to liven it up."

"Is that really the worst thing you did?"

"One of them. Your turn."

"I don't do bad things."

"Now that's not fair. You agreed to play, made me confess, and then you say that. Nuh-uh, there's got to be something."

She grimaces. "I stole gum from the Summerdale Mart." That's the small grocery store in town. "The sugar kind that blows big bubbles. My parents would never buy it for me."

"Did jolly old St. Nick catch you?" The store is run by Nicholas, a man in his sixties with white hair and a full beard, who resembles Santa.

She claps a hand to her forehead. "That was the worst part. I was seven and still believed in Santa. I was so sure he was the real Santa, and I thought I'd never get presents for Christmas again. I confessed and gave it back the next week, minus three pieces. Dad was so embarrassed he paid extra for it, and then I had no TV for a month."

"No TV? Horrors."

She laughs, a throaty sound that's so sexy. "It was horrible. I was addicted to *Speed Dawg*." That's a racing cartoon with dogs.

"No more *Speed Dawg*. Anything else?"

"Nah, I was pretty much a follow-the-rules kid."

"I was bad as much as I could get away with."

She faces front. "I could see that about you."

I bump her shoulder with mine. "I suspect you're shy. Is that true?"

She stares at me. "No, why would you say that?"

"You don't flirt like most women."

She's quiet before muttering, "Sorry to disappoint you. It's probably why most guys see me as a buddy."

I lean close. "I'm not disappointed. I like that you're different."

Her eyes meet mine, and I get that jolt again. There's definitely something here. "Oh," she says.

I have the urge to kiss her, but I restrain myself. Too soon.

She smooths her hair back, her lashes fluttering down. "You're the first guy to think it's good that I'm not like other women."

"I love that."

She gazes into my eyes. *Thunderbolt*. It's real.

∽

Sloane

Caleb's walking me to my car through the dark parking lot after our first date. I'm quiet, but my mind is whirling. I had a nice time tonight. He seems sincere, and he's such a cheerful guy full of good humor it's easy to relax around him. He did screw up, embarrassing me with Kayla, but he apologized. He's actually jealous of Max. I told him we were friends. Maybe Caleb just feels that strongly about me, which kind of makes me feel all floaty.

I almost don't want the night to end, but I don't want to invite myself to his place after our first date. No matter how lusty he makes me feel. My place is out since I live with Dad for now. Anyway, I'm sure most women go home with him after a first date, and I don't want to be just another woman he forgets about the next day.

"Well, I guess this is good night," I say when we reach my car. "I'll see ya, maybe. If you want, or whatever."

Some skill with flirting would be good about now.

"C'mere," he says, giving my arm a tug. "Over here in the light, where I can see you better. Let's talk for a minute."

I follow. As soon as we step out of the shade of a large tree, the full moon shines on Caleb. His angular features look sharper, like he's carved from marble. His masculine beauty simply shines. Even his light brown hair takes on a golden halo. What does he see when he looks at me? A plain woman used to being the odd duck, or something more?

He steps closer, ducking his head closer to my level to meet my eyes. "I want to see you again."

How about now? No, no, I can't rush into his bed, even though he's so handsome and kind and likes everything about me that doesn't fit the mold anywhere else. I'm still floored that he's into me.

"Me too," I whisper. "See you again too, I mean. Obviously I see myself all the time." I wave my hands around. "Hello!"

He smiles. "You're funny."

"That was me flirting."

"Ah. Are you blushing too? Hard to tell in this light."

My cheeks heat. "No."

He tucks a lock of hair behind my ear, his fingers grazing my overheated cheek. My breath hitches at his touch. "Yeah, you are."

I gaze up at him in the moonlight, enthralled, completely tongue-tied.

"You're so beautiful," he murmurs.

I stiffen. Here I was falling for all his sincerity, and now he's giving me lines. "You say these flattering things, and I'm sure lots of women fall—"

He leans close, the words hot against my lips. "I want *you*." He cradles my face with both hands, and the world falls away.

"What're you doing?" I ask inanely.

His voice is low, soothing. "I want you to fall the way I fell the first time I got close enough to really see you." His lips meet mine in a soft brush, sending a rush of pleasure through me. And then another brush, gentle, like I'm something precious. He deepens the kiss, and my knees go weak. It's the most delicious, erotic kiss of my life. My fingers curl into his shirt, keeping him close, returning the kiss with equal enthusiasm.

He breaks the kiss. "Thunderbolt," he murmurs, stroking my cheek.

More pretty words I don't understand. It sure sounds nice. I drop my hand from his chest, but I can't seem to move away.

He takes my hand. "I know it's not how the game is played, but I'm really into you."

I stare at him. No guy has ever said anything like that to me and definitely not the first time we went out. He's almost too good to be true. "Why?"

"You're beautiful, smart, and so unlike every other woman I meet." He takes my hand and places it over his heart, which is thumping hard. "I feel something. Here."

My mouth goes dry. The proof is right under my palm. I nearly cave, wanting nothing more than to throw my arms around him and kiss him until we're both breathless, but I can't. Part of me loves what he's saying; part of me suspects he's just that good at saying what women want to hear. I need to be smart about this.

I back up a step. "I'm a challenge. The moment you get what you want from me, you'll walk away."

"You mean sex? Sloane, honey, I can get that anywhere."

I scowl. "No kidding. I'm sure you're surrounded by scantily clad models with big tits every Tuesday."

"Today's Tuesday."

And I'm flat chested.

I narrow my eyes. "You know what I mean."

He steps closer, his voice soft by my ear. "I won't have sex with you until you agree to marry me."

I jolt. "Marry you!"

His eyes are intent on mine. "That's right. Commitment before we take that step."

"You're crazy. I'm not going to marry you. I barely know you."

"Not yet. You're also not having sex with me."

I stare at him, my gaze drifting to his mouth, his corded masculine neck, the wide expanse of shoulders. Oh, he's good because now it's all I can think about. Now I *want* to have sex with him.

I grab his head and pull him down to me for a passionate kiss. He returns it, his strong arm wrapping around my waist, pulling me up against his body, my toes barely trailing the ground. I never want this kiss to end. He is the king of all kissers, and I don't even care how he got this way because I can't stop wanting more.

"Oh! Is that Sloane and Caleb?" a feminine voice asks from a distance.

We break apart suddenly, facing Kayla and Adam on their way to their car. The worst part is, I'm not even embarrassed. I'm *irritated* by the interruption. All I can think about is getting back to kissing Caleb. I've never felt this kind of urgency before.

"Night," Caleb calls hoarsely.

Adam lifts a hand in farewell.

"Night!" Kayla calls cheerfully. "See you Thursday, Sloane!"

"See ya then!" I call, her cheerful friendliness warming me. She seems sincere, even if Caleb nudged her in my direction. It's hard to be insulted by his interference when she's so nice.

As soon as they get into their car, I turn to Caleb. "I want you." *Screw first-date protocol.*

He grazes his thumb over my lower lip. "Glad it's mutual."

"I'm staying with my dad. Let's go to your place."

"That's fine as long as you remember the rules. You have to agree to marry me before we have sex."

"Right." If he's using reverse psychology, it's totally working because now sex is all I can think about. Probably doesn't help that I haven't had sex since I hooked up with my former coworker, an English teacher, who recited Shakespeare sonnets as romantic foreplay. Unfortunately, that was the height of excitement for our entire encounter, which was over faster than a sonnet.

"I mean it," he says.

I nod. "Address?"

"I live in the apartment over Summerdale Sweets. Jenna and I switched places when she got engaged to Eli."

"Cool." It's just down the street, and the best part is he lives alone. "See ya there." I grab the key fob to my car out of my purse and unlock the car.

He reaches out to open the car door for me, surprising me. "I'm not playing around here, Sloane."

6

I pause, letting the words sink in. "Okay."

He nods once and shuts the door for me. I shiver and start the car, easing my way out of the lot and heading over to Summerdale Sweets.

I park in the street in front of the bakery. Dad sometimes picks up donuts or muffins for us to enjoy at work, but I haven't stopped by the shop. I should, especially since Jenna and I will be working on the Winterfest committee together starting tomorrow night.

I get out of the car, breathing in the crisp night air. Just down the road at the top of a hill is the old cemetery of the Presbyterian church. Most of the tombstones are from the eighteenth century, some of them listing to the side. I like to sit on the stone bench under the shade of a large oak tree there. It's kind of my secret place I go when I need some alone time. Some people might find it creepy, but I find it peaceful.

A few moments later, Caleb pulls into the driveway and gets out. I point across the street. "Ghosts ever bother you here?"

He turns to look across the street and turns back to me. "Actually, I go up there to keep them company sometimes. There's a stone bench—"

"Under the old oak tree. That's my secret getaway spot."

He walks over to me, taking my hand in his. One corner of his mouth kicks up. "Are you kidding me?"

"No," I say slowly. "That's my spot."

"That's *my* spot. How did I never run into you there?"

My jaw drops. I can't believe he's been hanging there too. "I usually go after work around sunset, only when I need some alone time. When I was in high school, I went there almost every day after school."

He gives my hand a squeeze. "Growing up, I used to sneak out of the house at midnight to visit. At first, I hoped to meet a ghost, and then it just became someplace where I could think."

I immediately wonder if he was hoping the ghost of his mother would visit him, but don't want to bring up a painful memory. It's common knowledge around town that his mom died in a car accident when he was young. I think his family went to the Presbyterian church, though there's no recent graves. They ran out of room more than a hundred years ago.

He continues, looking over at it. "I went up there again for the first time in a long time after I moved in here."

"That's what's so great about it. It's there when you need it."

He lifts my hand and kisses the knuckles, his eyes intent on mine. "Agreed." He guides me by the hand to the outside stairs leading to his apartment. "I have to warn you. Huckleberry will bark ferociously. He's a fantastic watchdog and looks scary as hell. He won't bite though."

"It's hard to be scared of a dog named Huckleberry."

His dog starts barking right on cue as we approach the front door. The deep-throated fierceness does give one pause.

"Glad I'm not a robber," I say.

"It's me," Caleb announces before unlocking the door. "Back it up." He grabs hold of the dog's collar, making room for me to step inside, and turns on the light. Huckleberry is a Siberian husky with blue eyes and a light gray coat with black markings.

"Hello, Huck," I say.

He lunges toward me, but Caleb has him tight by the

collar. "Sit," he commands. As soon as Huck sits, Caleb says to me, "You can pet him now."

I let Huck sniff my hand, and then reach back to scratch him behind the ear. "I love dogs, cats too, but Dad's allergic, so we could never have a pet."

"You can enjoy mine as long as you call him by his rightful name."

"Why Huckleberry?"

He pets his head vigorously, and Huck's tongue lolls in a doggy smile. "Because he's a goofball. He's a Huckleberry." He goes for a leash hanging on a hook near the door. "I'm going to take him for a quick walk. Make yourself at home." He snaps the leash on, and they head out the door.

I look around. It's not quite the bachelor pad I expected. It's actually kinda homey. I wonder if this is Jenna's furniture since they switched places. There's a gray sectional sofa with a long chaise lounge on one end, a few wooden end tables, a coffee table, and a TV on a small stand. The walls are painted a cream color. A collage of black-framed photos on the wall above the sofa catches my attention.

I walk over, expecting to see modeling photos from his work. It's all his family. His parents and the five kids are gathered in front of the Christmas tree. Caleb's beaming in the top left photo, probably around three. His hair is nearly blond. Oh, nice. Every photo is Christmas, same pose in front of the tree. You can see the kids growing up, and his parents with their arms around each other, looking happy. There's six pictures in total. They stop when Caleb's still little, maybe eight if these are one a year. If I remember correctly, that's when his mom died. Rather than keep up with the pictures, he stopped them here. There's something both sad and sweet about that.

I take off my coat and hang it on a hook by the door. Across from the living room area, there's a circular wrought-iron café table with two chairs. It looks small in the dining area. Through an archway is the kitchen. I look past the living room in the other direction, where there's a hallway that must lead to his bedroom.

Well, I'm not going to be presumptuous and just go in there and get naked, waiting for him. No matter how much I want him. That would be rude. I think. Or would that be seductive and sexy? I wish I had female friends to ask this kind of thing. The few times I've asked guy friends, they laughed their asses off and informed me all I had to do was say I wanted to fuck and it was a done deal. Even *I* know that's too forward on a first date. I don't want to scare him off.

I take a seat on the sofa and lean back, trying to look relaxed and comfortable. Like I seduce guys in a sexy way all the time.

The front door pops open, and Huckleberry races toward me, panting and happy. "Hi!" I pet him. His fur is cold from being outside. He bumps up close, his plumed tail curling up and wagging.

"Huckleberry, sit," Caleb orders. The dog instantly obeys, looking at him. "Good boy, good sit." He gives him a treat from his jacket pocket and looks at me. "I hired a trainer to teach me how to work with him. This dog is so smart and eager to please he got the hang of all the commands in a month. Watch how smart he is. Huckleberry, get the monkey."

Huckleberry trots to a large wicker basket in the far corner of the dining area and starts pulling out dog toys. Kongs, rope toys, a neon green frisbee, and then he grabs a purple monkey and runs to Caleb, dropping it at his feet.

"Impressive," I say.

"Watch this." Caleb feeds him a treat, praising him, and crouches down to him. "Get the yellow ball."

Huckleberry runs back and retrieves it from the basket, dropping it at Caleb's feet.

"That dog's got talent," I say, impressed. "He can even tell colors."

Caleb bites back a smile.

"Wait a minute." I walk over to the toy basket. There's two yellow balls in there. The only color. "Not so tough when they're all yellow."

Caleb grins. "You would've been impressed if you hadn't

peeked. He mostly sees the world in yellows and blues, though." He gives Huckleberry a rub on his side. "Good boy, showing off your smarts for us." He stands. "He also does this funny thing where he puts his own leash in his mouth and walks himself. I didn't teach him that trick. He thought of it all by himself. Can I get you anything?"

"I'm good." I lean down to pet Huckleberry's side, and he licks my face, surprising me. "Blech. Doggy kiss."

"Hope you don't mind if I eat. I didn't have dinner." He walks into the kitchen, and Huckleberry follows at a fast trot.

Geez, now I feel bad. Caleb probably thought we were going to have dinner together at The Horseman Inn. He did ask me if I wanted something to eat when we were there. I only committed to a drink because I was so uncertain about him. Guess I messed up there.

I follow him to the kitchen. "I didn't realize you hadn't eaten."

"No problem. I've got leftovers. I'll just heat them up. You can join me at the table. You want wine? I've got that, vodka, or water. Pick your poison."

"Water's fine. I'll get it."

I start looking through cabinets, and he comes up behind me, reaching over my head for the glass. He grins down at me. "Here you go."

I turn to face him, our bodies pressed close, the heat intoxicating. "Caleb."

He runs a finger down my nose. "I want to get to know you. Tell me everything."

I stare at his mouth, longing for another kiss. "There's nothing to tell. I grew up in Summerdale, moved away for college, spent four years at a job I didn't like, and now I'm home again."

He kisses me, a quick hard kiss. "You can do better than that." He shifts away, opening the refrigerator and pulling out a bowl of something, which he puts in the microwave.

I help myself to water at the sink. "I saw your family photos at Christmas. They were sweet. It's cool to see how the kids change in the photo, but your parents look the same. Happy."

"Happy and tired, I'm sure. They had five kids, and we were *not* angels. Dad ran The Horseman Inn, a longtime Robinson venture, and Mom was a nurse."

My mom was a salesclerk and then my manager until I thwarted her vicarious dreams by turning awkward. I keep that to myself.

A few minutes later, we shift over to his bistro table. Caleb's eating chicken stir-fry with rice. I sip my water, staring at the Christmas pictures.

After a while, I ask him, "Do the pictures make you feel better or worse at Christmas?" It's only two and a half weeks until Christmas.

He looks over his shoulder at them. "It reminds me that my parents are still part of us, which makes me feel good. It would be dumb to keep pictures up that make me sad."

"True."

"Mom died when I was eight, a few days after Christmas. Her car spun out on black ice when she was on her way to work at the hospital."

"So sorry."

He nods. "Thanks. Christmas was never the same after that, but I had my memories. Dad put up these pictures every Christmas to make it feel like she was part of things. I was the only one who wanted them after Dad died."

He's an orphan. I have the sudden urge to hug him. His dad didn't die until more recently, probably two years ago. I remember him from The Horseman Inn when I visited home.

I study him for a moment. He has such a naturally cheerful demeanor, it's hard to imagine what he's been through losing both parents relatively young. "It's good that you had all those siblings to keep you company. I'm an only child."

"Oh, yeah? Must've been quiet at your house."

"It was."

He nods. "I was lucky to have them. After Mom died, Dad stepped up, trying to be everything we needed, and my older sister, Sydney, she was kinda like a second mom to me. My older brothers looked out for me too. I survived. I figure you're close with your dad since you like working with him. How about your mom? She left town a while back, right?"

My least favorite topic of conversation, though I don't imagine he liked sharing what he just did. "Before the divorce, when I was very young, I felt close to her. Afterward, not so much."

"Your dad got custody, that's unusual."

I shrug. "Mom left the country. She didn't really take to the mothering thing."

"That's terrible."

I hold up a hand. "It worked out great. Dad and I have more in common and, if that hadn't happened, I never would've apprenticed to the world's greatest mechanic. I love my job there."

"You think you'll stick around Summerdale?"

"Definitely." I press my lips together. "Crap. Don't tell my dad that. He's eager for me to move on to a real career. He won't hear me when I say this is what I want."

"Maybe he'll come around when he realizes how indispensable you are." He smiles, and I find myself smiling back. He runs his thumb along my cheek, gazing into my eyes for a breathtaking moment. I'm enthralled.

He kisses me, a tender kiss that makes me want to crawl into his lap. He breaks the kiss and stands, his fingers trailing along my jaw as he tips my face up. He leans down and kisses me again.

I smile dreamily.

He gazes at me for an intense moment before turning away abruptly. "I'll wash up, and then we'll get down to business." He heads to the kitchen.

Huckleberry nearly knocks over the table, running out from under it to follow Caleb.

Business. Hmm…

He must mean sex. He kissed me right before he said it, we had a very hot makeout session in the parking lot, and he invited me to his place for more privacy. It's the only logical conclusion. I'm glad he's made this seduction thing so nice and clear for me.

He leaves his dishes in the dishwasher, winks at me, and heads down the hall. I assume to brush his teeth. Well, I'll just go wait for him in his bed. I can follow a seduction signal when I see it. The wink on top of the previous signals gives me confidence.

I put my water glass in the dishwasher and head down the hallway, where Caleb just disappeared. The bedroom door's closed. Huckleberry sits just outside it.

"Watch out," I say, nudging him back and squeezing through the doorway, quickly shutting it behind me. Don't want a dog in bed with us.

The bathroom door is closed. Great. That gives me time to prepare. I look around. His bedroom is sparse. Just a king-sized bed with a navy comforter and a gray cushioned head-board, a couple of wood and iron nightstands, and a tall chest of drawers. He must keep most of his clothes hanging in the closet. I'm impressed that he's neat. Dad always has clothes lying around and never bothers folding clean laundry, just pulls stuff straight from the basket.

Huckleberry whines from the other side of the door.

"Shh, it's okay," I tell him. I'm not doing anything nefarious in here to alarm a dog. Ha-ha. I quickly strip and dive under the covers. Ooh, the sheets must be silk. I wiggle down into them. They're light blue, and the effect of all the blue and gray bed coverings is so relaxing. I probably should turn off the overhead light and just leave on the nightstand lights.

I hear the water running in the bathroom. Okay, I've got time. I turn on the nightstand light and dash out of bed to the light switch by the door.

Huckleberry's paw appears under the door as he whines. I push it back. "Shh, go to sleep."

Ruf! Ruf! Ruf! He scratches at the door.

"Huckleberry, sit," I whisper fiercely through the door. I glance back toward the bathroom. Still closed.

Ruf! Ruf! And then it gets worse. Huckleberry howls over and over and over.

Damn, he's loud. I glance around and notice there's a dog bed in the corner next to the nightstand. Huckleberry must think it's bedtime, and he's been left out.

I dash for the dog bed, which is a large blue plaid beanbag with cream fleece on top. I rush back to the door and open it, shoving it toward him. Huckleberry grabs the end in his mouth and wriggles his head side to side.

"Don't eat it. You're supposed to sleep in it. Let go." I try to pull it from his mouth, but he lowers his back half for better leverage and hangs on. I just want to set it in the living room so he won't be alarmed for his owner by any bedroom noises.

Boy, is his jaw strong. "If I let go, will you take it to the living room?" I'm negotiating with a dog named Huckleberry.

He shakes his head, nearly pulling the bed from my grip. I dig my heels in, leaning back a bit. Suddenly he lets go and barks. I fall backwards—

Right into Caleb's arms. *Oh God*. Heat flashes through me in utter mortification. I was so caught up in our tug-of-war I didn't hear the bathroom door open.

Caleb grins down at me. "Why're you fighting Huckleberry for his bed?"

I straighten, keeping my back to him. "It's nice of you not to mention I'm naked fighting Huckleberry for his bed."

Caleb turns on the overhead light. "That part I like."

I dash to the side of the bed and pull my sweater back on, not bothering with the bra. The sweater's long enough to cover all the pertinent parts. Huckleberry races over, grabs my black panties, and takes off.

"Hey! Those are mine!" I'm not up for a pants-less dog chase with Caleb as a witness, so instead I pull my jeans on commando and work my bra on under the sweater. What a naughty dog.

Caleb looks me up and down from across the room. "Would it be out of line to say you look better without clothes?"

I freeze, torn between embarrassment and the gleaming

look of approval in his eyes. I just know he's seen many, many beautiful women both in his line of work and in his social life.

"I don't mind hearing it," I admit.

He closes the distance and wraps his arms around me. "I'd say those panties are toast." He strokes my hair soothingly, subtly conveying he understands how screwy everything got with my premature nakedness and my losing battle with a determined Siberian husky.

I rest my forehead against his chest. "This was supposed to be a sexy seduction."

He tips my chin up. "I'm hooked. Trust me."

Huckleberry races by with my panties and jumps on the bed, digging into the blanket and managing to lift it enough to hide my panties under the blanket. He lies down promptly, panting and looking mighty proud of himself.

"At least I know they're safe," I quip.

Caleb laughs and walks over to the bed. "Huckleberry, off." The dog immediately jumps off the bed and waits eagerly for the next command. Caleb rescues my panties and holds them up by the waistband with both hands. They look weirdly tiny in his hands. "At least they're all in one piece. I'll wash them for you."

"They're dead to me now. Just throw them out."

He slingshots them toward me, and I step aside. *So much for seduction.*

I have to know. "What did you mean when you said we'd get down to business?"

A smile plays over his lips. "Talking."

Major miscalculation. Guess I'll just slink on home now.

I cross my arms, looking everywhere but at him. "Oh."

"Would you feel better if I took my shirt off?"

7

I uncross my arms, my mouth going dry. "Yes, please."

He pulls his shirt off in a quick two-handed move that makes his muscles flex. My pulse races. This is *much* better. In fact, faced with the most gorgeous example of the male body I've ever seen, my former mortification fades into the background. It helps that I'm completely dressed (minus my panties), and he's on display just to even the playing field. A kind, sexy gesture on his part. His skin is golden, defined with sculpted muscle from his rounded shoulders down the length of his arms, his pecs, his abs. A light trail of hair disappears under the waistband of his jeans.

I lick my lips. "Do you do a lot of shirtless photo shoots?"

"Some. Or sometimes with the shirt open."

He lies down on the bed and opens the covers to me. I don't hesitate and dive in fully dressed.

I throw the covers over my head impulsively. Guess I'm not quite ready to show skin after my earlier display. "Can you turn out the light?" I ask, my voice muffled from under the covers.

"But I've already seen your sweet little body."

True. I'd probably relax if we started kissing again, but then I remember our furry witness. "Is Huckleberry staring at us?"

Something leaps on top of me, and I squeak, yanking the covers off my face. It's not Huckleberry. Caleb's trapped me under him, his arms and legs on either side of mine.

"I'm trapped," I protest.

He cups my jaw. "Surrender, darling." He kisses me. Long, deep kisses that make me forget everything but the heat and weight of him, the taste of him, the firm press of his lips.

He shifts, his mouth trailing along my neck, his teeth scraping against me. I shiver. He pulls me up so he can take my shirt off, next my bra, and then pushes me back down on the mattress. Now we're both shirtless in jeans. He caresses my breasts, bringing the nipples to peaks, which he then sucks, an insistent tugging that makes my hips move restlessly as desire pools between my legs.

I let my hands roam freely over him, reveling in the hard planes of muscle, the restrained power. His crew-cut hair is strangely soft and spiky at the same time. His mouth meets mine again in a lingering kiss.

He lifts his head. "We should stop."

"We should not stop." I unbutton my jeans and wriggle out of them. Now I'm completely naked since Huckleberry took my panties. I don't even care where that naughty dog is as long as he doesn't interrupt.

He keeps his gaze on my face. "I told you we weren't going to have sex until you agree to marry me."

My jaw drops. "Are you being serious right now? You invited me into your bed. You kiss me like you mean business and not the talking kind." No wonder I miscalculated earlier. *Mixed signals much?*

"Thunderbolt," he murmurs, which makes no sense.

I have no time to think on that because his hand trails down my bare stomach, and every muscle in my body tightens in anticipation. He shifts, running his hand down my side, over the curve of my small hip. He kisses my hip. "You have the sweetest little curves."

I close my eyes. "I don't think it's fair to bring me to your bed and then, you know, talk about marriage when there's more pressing needs right now."

His lips brush against mine. "What kind of need are we talking about?"

I grasp the back of his neck and stare directly into his eyes. "Very urgent needs."

His hand makes a slow trail from my hip to the crease of my thigh and then down my inner thigh. He watches my expression as he moves. "Has it been a while for you?"

"Yes." I don't ask how long it's been for him, but he shares anyway, his hand stilling on my upper thigh.

"Me too. I decided I was tired of meaningless empty sex."

I'm sure his version of a long time is much shorter than my own. Hold up. If he's tired of meaningless sex, then what is he doing in bed with me on our first date?

Is us being together deeply meaningful to him? Is that what the thunderbolt is? Like, love at first sight?

Is that why he's talking about marriage?

This is nuts!

I'm about to tell him that when his mouth covers mine, coaxing mine open and then exploring inside. I melt into the mattress. And then his fingers, his magnificent fingers, home in on pleasure central, and my legs fall open in complete surrender.

He kisses me over and over while his fingers draw me up, up, up, in a tight spiral of pleasure. And then he watches my expression as his fingers work magic. I can't look away, mesmerized by the intensity of his eyes, somehow both holding me close and making me come apart. Something deep passes between us, a rush of emotion, a recognition of souls.

I shudder as the orgasm hits in a rush of pleasure. His mouth covers mine, swallowing my soft cries.

He lifts his head. "Beautiful, you're so beautiful, Sloane."

I blink back unexpected tears. I actually believe him.

∽

Caleb

I've got a naked sexy woman in my bed, and now I don't

know what to do with her. She can't stay because the temptation will be too strong for me. I drew a line in the sand, mostly because I wanted her to believe in my sincerity. The only way to know for sure she's the One is to spend time getting to know each other. Sloane checks all the boxes—smart, beautiful, capable, sexy. And there's something more. She's not fake in any way. Not with layers of cosmetics or her manner. Everything about her is straightforward and honest. Even when she's awkward, it's adorable because it's real.

And the fact that we share a secret place in Summerdale, where I've never seen anyone else, must mean something too. After Mom passed, I felt closest to her there, even though she's buried outside town. She took us to the Presbyterian church when we were kids. Could Mom have sent Sloane my way?

All of these signs—the jolt, the easy compatibility, the shared secret spot in town—does that make Sloane the one I've been waiting for? I'm leaning toward yes. Still, I don't want to rush her. Dad proposed to Mom on their first date. I'm not proposing. I'm just saying let's not have sex until we're there. A proposal for the future us.

Am I nuts?

I get out of bed and look for Huckleberry. He's made himself comfortable, lying on top of Sloane's clothes. I slide them out from under him and shake them out, brushing them off. "Not too bad. Just a little fur on them."

"Are you kicking me out?" Her voice hits a high note.

"No, you can stay. It just seems safer if we're both dressed."

She grabs her clothes and pulls them on quickly. "I know when I've overstayed my welcome."

"Hey, it's not that. I just don't want to rush this."

"Totally get it." She rolls out of bed on the other side to avoid me.

I walk around and meet her there, grabbing my shirt from the nightstand and pulling it on. "It doesn't take much to set you off. You have a temper."

Her amber eyes flash. My heart jolts, thumping harder. "I don't have a temper."

"You're racing to leave because you think I don't want you here."

She lifts her chin. Her hair is a rumpled mess from my fingers and the mattress. "I'm not mad that you want me to go. It's fine. I get it, okay?"

I curl my fingers around the back of her neck, drawing her close. "I agree it would be easier on me if you left because, if you haven't noticed, I'm pretty turned on. But that doesn't mean you have to go. I'll calm down eventually."

She glances at my crotch, which is straining against my jeans. "Oh, it really is just bulging there. Should I, uh, help you out?"

"No," I grit out.

She meets my eyes, a determined glint in them. "I can't marry you, you know, so you might as well drop that whole *no sex before marriage* thing."

"Why not? Are you secretly married to someone else?"

"No."

"Don't tell me you're not eighteen yet."

She laughs. "Now you're being ridiculous."

"What a relief."

She pushes my chest. "You know I'm a year older than you."

I push her hair back from her face, lean down, and kiss her cheek. "Then I don't see the problem."

She pats my shoulder. "This was nice. Thanks." She walks toward the door.

I stare after her, torn between letting her go and asking her to stay. I seem to be alone in this thunderbolt situation. Dad did propose to Mom three times before she agreed. Maybe Sloane just needs time to catch up. Or maybe I'm imagining this whole thing. Dad's the only Robinson to believe in love at first sight for the One. Was it just family legend? Only one way to know for sure.

"Dinner tomorrow night," I call.

She stops and turns, her eyes meeting mine. *Jolt.* "I have the Winterfest committee meeting tomorrow night."

"And I have beginners karate class. Before that. I'll meet you for a quick bite."

She shakes her head. "Aren't you—don't you want..."

"What?"

She throws her hands up. "This is my nice outfit. Fair warning. This is as good as it gets."

I shake my head. She's worried that I'm used to models, which isn't far from the truth, but I've learned to look deeper.

She gestures toward her legs. "And I have a pencil skirt too, which I hate wearing in the winter because it makes me cold."

I prowl toward her. Her eyes widen, and she backs up a step. I wrap an arm around her waist and walk her back to the wall, pinning her against it.

Her eyes dilate, her breath coming harder. "What're you doing?" she asks breathlessly.

I speak near her ear. "Didn't I tell you that no clothes is the best look for you?"

She nods. There's a pulse point beating rapidly in her delicate throat. I press my mouth there and hear her sigh. My lips curve up. The chemistry between us works. It's a promising start.

I lift my head to meet her eyes directly. "You don't have to change who you are for me. Wear whatever makes you comfortable."

She stares at me, her lips parted.

I give her one last kiss. "See you tomorrow night for dinner. I'll text you the details."

She nods and turns, heading for the front door. I walk out with her, retrieving her purse from where she left it by the sofa. I help her on with her coat.

She looks up at me, her cheeks a rosy pink. "Goodnight, Caleb. This was really nice." Her voice is soft with a touch of longing.

It takes everything I have to let her go. I kiss her forehead. "Night."

She leaves, and I let out a breath.
Huckleberry trots in with her panties in his mouth.
"Give me those!"

Sloane

I walk into Summerdale Pizza, and Caleb is already there, standing just inside. I'm suddenly tongue-tied. This man saw me naked. He gave me an explosive orgasm, told me good night, and now we're having a casual date of pizza.

"Hello," he says warmly.

Heat spreads through me just from his voice. It's like his warmth is contagious. "Hi. I didn't think models ate pizza."

"I'll work it off with karate classes tonight. Drew and I usually spar afterward too. He's a great workout partner. Former Army Ranger."

"Cool. Yeah, I heard he was. I'd be nervous to fight with him, even just for sparring."

He takes my hand and walks with me to the counter. "Nah. He's my big bro. Besides, he's got iron control. He was the leader of his team because they could depend on him to keep a cool head."

I suppress a shiver at the calm deadly soldier image that comes to mind. "I guess that's good."

"Yeah, what can I get you?"

"I'll take a slice of pepperoni, thanks."

He orders for me and then gets himself a salad and a slice of white pizza with spinach.

I study his profile with its perfect angles and flawless skin. "You're one of those weirdos who drink green smoothies, aren't you?"

His hazel eyes meet mine. "What you put on the inside shows on the outside. You like the results, don't you?"

"You're full of yourself."

He leans close, whispering in my ear, "Your blush gives you away, darling."

"I'm not blushing." It's weird that he calls me darling. I'm not *darling* at all. That implies a cute sweet little thing.

Sal, a middle-aged guy with thinning brown hair, pipes up from behind the counter, "You're red from cheek to cheek, honey. What's this guy saying in your ear?"

"Nothing," I say, even more embarrassed.

"She's shy," Caleb says.

Sal pulls the collar of his red polo shirt up, ducking his head. "Then you need to coax her out of her shell. Like a turtle."

Puh-lease. "I'm going to grab us a table." I pull some napkins from the dispenser on the end of the counter and take a table by the front window.

A few minutes later, Caleb sits across from me with our pizza on paper plates. "I might have to revise my opinion on your shyness. After all, you stripped for me on our first date."

My cheeks flame. "Would you keep your voice down?"

"What? It's just us in here. Sal's back by the ovens. He can't hear us."

I take a bite of pizza and chew. "Never bring that up again. Pretend it didn't happen."

"But every time I look at you, I see under your clothes with that X-ray vision you gave me." He opens his water bottle. "You know, because of the naked thing."

I lean forward. "Stop saying naked."

"Naked."

I pretend strangle him. He laughs, grabs my wrists, and kisses each of them. My breath stutters out. How did I manage to get the attention of this gorgeous man? And it's not just his looks. His whole personality is like a ray of sunshine—cheerful, bright, generously shining all over me. He's almost too perfect.

He takes a bite of pizza and smiles. There's a piece of spinach stuck in his front teeth. I don't say a word. He's finally not so perfect, and that makes me relax.

He tells me about his brother Eli, who's getting married in a little over three weeks on New Year's Eve in what's supposed to be a small ceremony at his sister Sydney's house with her husband, Wyatt. The numbers are getting out of hand between their families, close friends, and the dogs that Jenna insists have to be there. Jenna believes she's a dog mom, and that means her pit bull, Mocha, needs to be there, as well as Eli's pit bull, Lucy, and since Sydney and Wyatt already have two dogs, now they're thinking of setting up a doggie play area right outside the large windows of the ceremony area. The dogs will be dressed in formal wear, of course.

He drinks some water and runs his tongue along his teeth. "Think I should bring Huckleberry?"

Damn, he's perfect again. No more spinach in his teeth.

I shake my head. "I keep telling you, the other dogs will make fun of him for that ridiculous name. You can't let him show his face with Huckleberry following him around." I take a bite of pizza and chew.

"How about you? Would you like to be my plus one?"

I nearly choke on my pizza. I finish chewing and swallow. "You said it's a small family wedding. I don't belong there."

"I already asked Jenna, and she said it's okay to bring you."

My eyes widen. "You did?"

"Yeah, earlier today."

"Do you think we'll be together in three weeks?" I blurt.

He grabs my pizza and puts it on his plate. "No more pizza for you until you admit you're into me."

I stare at my pizza squished half on top of his slice. Kinda like we were last night, all wrapped together in his bed. I lift my head to find his eyes intent on mine. He's serious about this. "How could any woman *not* be into you? You're like the ideal male specimen except for the fact that you talk crazy sometimes about thunderbolts and steal people's dinner."

He tilts his head. "Sorry, what was that?"

I lean across the table and whisper, "I'm into you. Can I have my dinner back now?"

He leans close, his eyes gleaming wickedly. "I know. I just wanted you to admit it."

I snatch my pizza back and take a ferocious bite.

"You can wear your pencil skirt to the wedding," he says.

I clap a hand on my forehead. I can't believe he remembered that was my only dressy outfit.

"Or I could take you shopping for a dress, or—" he holds up a finger "—even better, if you want some primo designer stuff, I have access to some wardrobe we could borrow."

Somehow I'm going to a family wedding with him. They'll think we're serious about each other, and this is only our second date. I can't believe Caleb is desperate for a girl-friend, so his talk of commitment and marriage must be specific to me. Uh, *hello*! Second date. Not only is he setting us up for way too high of expectations, but there's bound to be an inevitable fall. How can he be so sure we're meant to be together?

"Caleb, I think maybe we need to take a step back here."

"It's too fast."

"Well, yeah, I'm a little overwhelmed."

His expression shutters closed. "Got it."

Crap. I think I hurt his feelings.

"Let's just spend time together, casual, like now, okay?" I say. "This is good."

He leans back in his seat. "I won't be around this week-end. That's why I wanted to see you today. Friday I have a photo shoot in the city for a charity calendar, and I'll be spending the weekend getting a new model settled in at my apartment in the city." New York City being what locals call "the city."

"Wow. I didn't know you had an apartment in the city. Rent there is killer."

"The agency owns the apartment, and I stay there for free

in exchange for helping the new guys get settled in and making sure they stay out of trouble."

My heart softens. "So you're like a mentor to the younger models."

He lifts one shoulder in a casual gesture. "Yeah, I guess so. The agency trusts me to keep 'em on the straight and narrow."

I like that a lot. He's a good guy with his head on straight. "Cool. What's the charity calendar for?"

"It's my shoot, actually. A fundraiser for a new animal shelter here in Summerdale. Shirtless guys with their dogs." He flashes a smile, warming to his topic. "Dr. Russo, the vet, he's been taking in strays in a small space at his vet's office and helping them find homes. That's how I got Huckleberry. Huckleberry's owners moved and didn't want to take him with them. Anyway, Dr. Russo is trying to raise enough money to build a state-of-the-art shelter on the property behind the vet office."

He's bringing his modeling skills to a good cause. He's legit awesome. "That's great. If it's for a local cause, why didn't you ask local guys to pose with their dogs? Your brothers could pose shirtless. People would definitely fork over money to see that." *Especially Drew.* He might be scary in his stealth way, but there's no denying the man keeps spectacularly fit. I keep that to myself.

One corner of his mouth kicks up. "I'd be jealous if I didn't know you were so crazy about me that you got—" he mouths *naked* "—on our first date. Anyway, no. My brothers, hell, most people around here don't get what I do."

"What do you mean?"

He exhales sharply, his sunny demeanor dimming. "They just don't think much of it. Like it's a shallow thing. So what if I'm cheerful and the camera loves me? That doesn't mean I'm shallow. It's just the optics. They don't get it."

"Have they actually called you shallow?" The way he talks about his older brothers, I assumed they supported him in all things.

He frowns. "In so many words. I don't get taken seriously for the most part. Youngest, the baby, floating through life with gobs of cash because I was blessed with good genes."

"Modeling is hard work."

He straightens, studying me. "It is. How do you know?"

I look away. "I heard. Or maybe I read it somewhere."

"It can be long grueling days, but obviously there's perks."

My mind immediately flashes to long-limbed models in bikinis. I keep my mouth shut.

"You could join me at the photo shoot. Jenna's been involved since she's helping with the shelter fundraiser. She'll be there to lend a hand wrangling the dogs while I wrangle the models. Twelve models and their dogs, one for every month."

Adrenaline spikes through me. I swore I'd never step foot on a modeling shoot again. I've got post-traumatic stress over it. For real. I don't need the reminder of what my life was like before my looks bailed on me, along with my mother. Not that I'm ugly now. I know I'm more of a plain Jane. I'm not the industry ideal, and my skin crawls just thinking about the reminder—lights, camera, the photographer directing the model.

"I'm, uh, not great with wrangling dogs," I say. "You saw me fight with Huckleberry over a dog bed."

He grins, his hazel eyes sparkling. He doesn't have to say it. He's thinking it—me *naked* fighting over a dog bed.

I jab a finger at him. "Don't say it."

He grabs my finger. "It would be great to have you there with me. We could hang out in the city after."

"I'd just be in the way."

"I want to see you when I get back. Sunday night."

How can I say no? Caleb has me taking all kinds of crazy chances with my heart. I nod.

He cups my cheek and kisses me. A warm glowy feeling bubbles up inside me. No man has ever so openly adored me like this. It's almost too good to be true.

A niggling voice of warning sounds in my mind. When something seems too good to be true, it usually is. I don't want to think about that. Right now everything feels magical.

9

Shortly after our dinner, I walk into the Summerdale library and head up to the second-floor loft space, where there's a glass-enclosed meeting room, along with some quiet study space and the librarian's office. I don't know what to expect from a Winterfest committee meeting. I typically contribute in quiet ways to the community—free math tutoring, fixing a car on a low- or no-payment plan, donating to the local fire department, EMTs, the library, everyone who keeps this place going on a voluntary or publicly funded basis. I'm not even sure *how* to help. I doubt math or cars will be involved here.

The Summerdale Winterfest (unironically named but funny to me, summer/winter) is usually in the dead of January, after all the excitement of the holidays has passed, and we're facing day after dreary day of cold gray winter. There's a parade around the lake, ice skating if the lake is frozen enough, a variety show at the Standing O theater in the big red barn, and food vendors from town along the lakeshore. My favorite memory as a kid was toasting marsh-mallows on the beach for s'mores. I froze my ass off, but those s'mores made it all worth it.

I peek into the meeting room. My third-grade teacher, Mrs. Ellis, is sitting there chatting with Nicholas, the guy who looks like Santa and owns the Summerdale Mart I stole gum from as a kid. It's impossible not to face your past when you move back home. Mrs. Ellis used to get mad that I missed so much school for modeling auditions and photo shoots. She used to tell me, in a stern voice that scared the crap out of me, that I needed to inform my mother that my education was more important than pictures. I always turned in my homework and kept up with the class, but she still gave me a bit of side-eye. At the time, I decided she was just a mean old lady, but in hindsight, she must've been looking out for me.

Audrey pops up by my side, her blue eyes as bright as her smile. Her long black hair is in a bun with pencils sticking out of it. Must've been a rough day at the library. "Go on in. I'll be there in a sec."

"Are you expecting more people?" I kinda want more of a buffer before approaching the room. Call me crazy, but I still feel a bit like that shoplifting kid who missed too much class time.

"Are you afraid of the General?" she whispers, her eyes dancing with amusement.

She must mean Mrs. Ellis. Nicholas is as cheerful as Santa normally. "Is that what people call her?"

She keeps her voice low. "My friends and I did. We saw her a lot because she's Harper's grandmother and raised her. She scared us girls. Even now I can't help standing up straighter around her. She comes off like a harsh taskmaster, but her heart's in the right place." Harper Ellis is a famous actress now. Everyone in town knows about her.

"I'm not scared so much as…slightly uncomfortable."

"Uh-huh, well, Jenna will be here soon, along with Levi." She smiles, shaking her head. "I'm still getting used to calling Levi the mayor, even though it's been four years. We grew up together, oh, and Mrs. Peabody from Summerdale Nursery School will be here. That's everyone."

"What about Sydney and Kayla?"

"They'll be jumping in to help at the event itself."

I'd thought this would be more like joining the fun group from ladies' night. I don't know Levi or Mrs. Peabody that well. Levi was ahead of me in school, and I didn't go to

Summerdale Nursery School. That's the stricter preschool run by the Presbyterian church. My parents sent me to the so-called "hippy" preschool run by the Episcopalians, who believed play was more important than learning letters and numbers. I think I would've liked the letters and numbers place better. Mom was a free spirit. I never quite got what she saw in Dad. Though I know why they got married—me. One unplanned pregnancy, a quickie wedding, followed by a divorce once Mom didn't have my modeling career to stick around for. I suppose it could've gone differently, but Dad's an old-fashioned traditional guy. He proposed the moment she announced she was pregnant.

Welp, here goes. I'm twenty-six years old, and there's no reason to be intimidated by my third-grade teacher or to feel guilty for my brief shoplifting career.

I step inside, and two sets of eyes stare at me. I suddenly want to apologize for not being a perfect student and also for being a delinquent. "Hi."

"Sloane Murray, good to see you involved," Mrs. Ellis says. "Come sit by me and tell me how you are."

Wow, the General sounds so warm and cordial. Maybe retirement agrees with her. It must be draining to order third graders around for decades. Mrs. Ellis is in her eighties, but she's still vibrant. She's wearing a blue scarf tied around her neck with a thick lavender wool sweater. Her white hair is short and spiky, her brown eyes sharp as ever.

Mrs. Ellis is at the head of the table, so I take the seat adjacent to her. Santa, I mean, Nicholas is across from me. He's a white-haired guy in his sixties with a full white beard and a round belly. He adds to the Santa image by wearing bifocals and a red shirt with suspenders. I guess he likes preserving his image for the kids around town. Most of us believed Santa lived in Summerdale, not the North Pole, even though he always said he was just Santa's helper.

"How's your dad?" Nicholas asks me.

"He's doing well. Busy at the garage. I'm helping him keep on top of things, and Max Bellamy is there part-time, too, just for the winter."

"What made you leave teaching?" Mrs. Ellis asks. "I've heard nothing but good things about you as a math tutor since you were in high school. Seemed like such a natural fit."

"I'm good at it, but I don't love it. I love working on cars."

She purses her lips. "Bet your dad's not happy about that after paying for college."

I incline my head. My modeling paid for part of it too, but I don't mention it since she never liked that I missed school to model. "He'd prefer it if I used my degree."

She taps the table. "Now I firmly believe in the power of a good education, but there's one thing raising Harper has taught me. Following your passion can be the most satisfying life imaginable. She's doing what she's meant to do, acting and even directing a bit now, and she positively glows with happiness. Of course that might also be helped along by her wonderful husband, Garrett. He's a *real man*, and I tell you, Garrett can fix anything! He's such a help around my house. Have you seen my great-granddaughter, Caroline?"

Before I can reply, still a little stunned by her warm enthusiasm, she picks up her phone from the table, taps rapidly, and then shows me picture after picture of baby Caroline. I'm a little surprised at her dexterity with the phone. I always thought of her as an old-fashioned technophobe. In third grade, we were the only classroom that still used the chalkboard instead of the screen that was synched to a laptop. Even the laptop, she barely touched.

She smiles at the phone screen, her eyes never leaving it. "She's five months old, already sitting up with just a little support on her back. And she smiles, oh, her smiles!"

I'm beginning to see why Mrs. Ellis is less intimidating now. Her great-granddaughter made her happy and mellowed her out. Caroline is a beautiful baby with wispy light brown hair and blue-green eyes. Her parents dress her in a variety of cute outfits with daisies, cherries, polka dots, various bright primary colors, always with coordinating tiny bows in her hair. I could totally see her in a commercial for diapers or baby food, but I wouldn't wish that life on any kid, no matter how nice it is to have money for college.

"Finally gave in to the cell phone craze," Nicholas says.

Mrs. Ellis doesn't miss a beat, still showing me pictures—there must be a thousand of them—while telling Nicholas, "I resisted at first, but then my son-in-law gave me a phone over Thanksgiving and showed me how easy it would be to share pictures and video chat with Caroline. He set it all up for me. It's important she sees and hears from me regularly. Technology has its place. Give me your number."

He does, saying it slowly and clearly, and she sends him a picture of Caroline.

He pulls his phone from his pocket in surprise. "What's this?"

"I just sent you her picture," she says. "Click accept and it'll be in your photos."

He taps his phone and stares in wonder. "Well, I'll be. How did you do that? I'll send you a picture of my cat, Noelle."

They get into an enthusiastic discussion of tech, based on everything her son-in-law has taught her—all the tricks—and I'm finally done admiring a baby I've never met. I do love kids, which is why I've always been a math tutor. Even when I was a full-time math teacher, I tutored underprivileged kids on Saturdays. So many kids fall behind in math, and it's the one subject that continually builds on itself. A shaky foundation makes for years of difficulty. I shore up the foundation.

The door opens, and we all look over. Audrey's holding the door for Jenna, who's on crutches. Her blond hair swings in her face as she makes her awkward way in.

"Jenna!" Mrs. Ellis exclaims. "What happened?"

"Sprained ankle," Jenna says. "Slipped on the ice this morning on the way to my car. The good news is, it's my left foot, so I can still drive. The best news is, I'm only on crutches for two weeks, and the boot comes off in time for my wedding."

She takes a seat next to me and sets her crutches against the table. "I need to talk to you after this," she says by my ear.

My eyes widen. *Me? What could Jenna possibly need to talk to me about?*

Levi walks in, wearing a plaid beige flannel shirt with khakis. A casual mayor. His longish brown hair is slicked back, and he has a trimmed beard. He took over after Mayor Perkins, who'd been mayor forever and died at eighty-seven.

He shakes my hand. "So good to have another volunteer. You work at the garage, right? Mr. Murray's daughter."

"Yes, Sloane Murray."

"Welcome. I'm Levi Appleton."

He shakes hands with Mrs. Ellis, who wants to know if he's getting enough to eat in his lonely bachelor house, and then shakes hands with Nicholas, who just smiles. Levi keeps Mrs. Ellis in suspense until, at her persistent questioning, he finally says he's eating takeout from the Chinese restaurant in town, which is healthy.

"You need to take better care of yourself, Levi," Mrs. Ellis says sternly. "A man your age should be thinking of settling down."

I guess she thinks the two go hand in hand. Taking care of himself will attract a mate. I think of Caleb and his healthy lifestyle, and my heart does a little flip. Might be something to that.

"Mmm-hmm," Levi says, taking out a notepad and pen from his leather satchel. I get the feeling they have this conversation weekly.

Audrey gestures for Mrs. Peabody to come in. The preschool director is a thin woman with pinched lips and her gray hair in a bun. After brief hellos all around, we get down to business. The committee fills me in on what they've done already, which is the usual stuff I remember from Winterfest as a kid, but now they're looking for new ideas.

"We should do something with dogs," Jenna says. "Something that would be a fundraiser for the shelter Dr. Russo wants to build. He still doesn't have enough money to break ground."

That's when I remember Jenna's involved in another fundraiser for the shelter, the photo calendar Caleb organized. They're shooting it on Friday. Is that what she wants to talk to me about?

An enthusiastic debate ensues over what to do with dogs and if it should be indoor or outdoor. The ideas range from dogsled races to a dog beauty contest to a dog parade. I think of Huckleberry and how Caleb bragged about how smart he is, picking up the right toys on command. Naughty too, but that could be funny.

I raise my hand for attention. "What about a Dog's Got Talent contest? There'd be an entry fee, and then the owners could show off whatever special thing their dog can do. Doesn't have to be anything big. Just something fun."

"That sounds awesome," Jenna says. "Everyone thinks their dog is the most special, but I know mine is. Mocha can balance a plush puppy on his head and walk all around the house, even upstairs, without it falling off."

"How did you find that out?" I ask.

"He had a mouth full of tennis balls and wanted the plush puppy too, but couldn't fit it in his mouth, so I put it on his head. He likes having a lot of toys to himself instead of sharing with Lucy, that's our other pit bull."

Mayor Levi grabs his pen and jots it down on his notepad. "I like it. Let's add that to the plan."

"I was thinking of moving beyond the usual bake sale," Jenna says. "My hot chocolate, brownies, and fudge are huge sellers in the winter. So-o-o we could have a chocolate festival!"

"Omigod, I love chocolate," Audrey says. "Yes. That sounds amazing."

Mrs. Peabody offers the idea of using the Presbyterian church addition for indoor games for kids, which everyone agrees with. And then Audrey throws out the most absurd idea.

"I thought it would be fun to have a snow king and queen with a coronation and a royal ball."

We all stare at her.

She continues. "I researched other communities' winter festivals online. It's a charitable thing. The official king and queen are chosen from nominated people based on their contribution to the community. Then the king and queen become Summerdale ambassadors, participating in local parades, fundraisers, festivals, and visit the schools for special occasions. It would be open to any age, as long as they're adults. What do you think? We'd sell tickets to the ball to cover the cost of renting a space and to raise money for the animal shelter."

"I love it!" Jenna exclaims.

Audrey beams. "I even thought of official titles—King Frost and Queen Snowflake."

Everyone enthusiastically agrees with the concept, except me. I keep quiet. It's not my place to squash ideas. I'm sure some people would find it fun. It sounds too close to a beauty pageant to me, having a king and queen. I had my share of kiddy pageants. That's how I got a modeling agent.

Mrs. Ellis takes over, sounding just like the general Audrey and friends secretly call her, as she barks out orders, assigning responsibilities for the logistics of all the new items on the agenda. I exchange an amused look with Audrey. And then the General puts me in charge of organizing the royal ball!

"But I don't know anything about royal balls," I protest.

"You're a quick study," Mrs. Ellis says. "Besides, all your modeling experience will surely be put to good use rounding up the king and queen. We should have a court, too, made up of honors students from the high school. See, Sloane, that's right up your alley too, working with high school students." The woman has a mind like a steel trap. Of all the kids she taught over the years, she still remembers I used to be a kid model.

"But—"

"You are here to contribute, are you not?" Mrs. Ellis demands, her sharp eyes boring into mine.

I sit up straighter. "Yes, ma'am."

"Good. Every person in this room has been assigned a task according to their natural abilities."

Since there's no task for fixing cars or teaching math, I don't have much recourse. It's not like I know anything about the other tasks either.

Her voice softens. "You might want to find another volunteer to help you. It's a big job."

With that, the meeting adjourns quickly. Nicholas walks Mrs. Ellis out, crooking his elbow for her to take, which she refuses despite limping from a bad hip.

Jenna grabs my arm. "Stick around."

I stay, watching Nicholas and Mrs. Ellis on their way out in the midst of an animated discussion. He's smiling; she looks stern.

After everyone files out, Jenna says, "Would you be willing to step in for me at the dog calendar photo shoot on Friday with Caleb? He says he already asked you to join him, and you didn't feel qualified to wrangle dogs, but I'm desperate. The shoot will be chaos without someone helping. If you keep them on leash, it should be workable. And before you ask, I'm asking you for two reasons—one, Caleb's into you. He told Eli, my fiancé, that you were the coolest woman he's ever met, and I thought that was so sweet."

I suck in air. *Me? Cool?*

She continues. "Caleb always did say exactly what he thinks. It would be good for you to see him in his element."

My gut does a slow roll. I don't want to do something that brings up so much past pain. The glaring lights, the camera with its all-seeing lens, the photographer shouting out directions. Mom coaching from the side: "Head high, big smile!"

Ugly duckling in reverse.

"Please consider it," Jenna says at my silence. "The second reason I'm asking you is because I already asked Sydney, Audrey, and Kayla, and they can't get away from work on Friday. Not that you're my last choice, it's just that I don't know you well enough to beg a favor, but here I am, begging. It'll probably run late. I'm hoping since you work for your dad and Max is there now too, you might be able to get some time off. It's for a good cause. And I'll owe you one. Free hot cocoa all winter, or whatever you want from my bakery."

I swallow hard, trying to push my awful memories away. "I'll think about it."

She lets out a breath. "Okay, but it's only two days away. If you can't do it, Caleb has to wrangle the dogs and manage the shoot by himself, which is really tough to do. Did I mention the man-candy factor? Twelve models. Though I'm sure Caleb is the best of the bunch." She elbows me.

"I mentioned to him that he could've used local guys instead of models, but Caleb didn't think his brothers thought much of his modeling. He says most people see him as just a pretty face."

"That's not true. Eli never said one bad thing about him being a model."

"Did he ever say a good thing?"

She looks thoughtful. "Hmm...not that I ever heard. He does tease him about drinking kale smoothies."

"He could just be sensitive about it." Or maybe he has a chip on his shoulder because he secretly fears he won't be accepted for who he is and what he likes to do. Sounds a little like someone I know. That gives me pause. Maybe Caleb is the odd duck in his family. His brothers have practical careers —a karate studio owner, a carpenter, and a cop. His sister runs the family restaurant.

"Ooh, I know," Jenna says. "How about tomorrow you visit Dr. Russo with me on your lunch break? I'm sure if you saw his setup and the animals he has waiting for adoption, you'd really get how important this is."

"That's not necessary."

She picks up her phone and taps over to a website, which shows the animals waiting for adoption. There's a mother-daughter calico cat pair, a senior citizen Boston terrier with pointy ears, and a yellow hound. The cats are curled up together in their kennel. The Boston terrier is wearing a bowtie, staring at the camera rather haughtily. The yellow hound's mouth is open in what seems like a happy smile as he looks off camera. My heart squeezes. They just need a little love.

"I suddenly want to take them all home with me," I say.

She throws an arm around my shoulders and gives me a sideways hug. "I knew you must have a heart of gold. Otherwise Caleb wouldn't be so gaga over you. Thank you! Do you want to tell Caleb the good news, or should I? You're doing it, right?"

"If it's okay with my dad to take Friday off." I ignore the churning in my gut. This is bigger than my personal trauma. This is for animals in need.

"How's Max?" she asks.

I'm surprised she asked. "Good."

She speaks in a conspiratorial tone. "There was a lot of tension between him and Audrey last Thursday at the bar. You think there's still something there?"

"I have no idea. He was cagey about it."

She glances around, probably for Audrey. "Why don't you invite him tomorrow night for ladies' night?"

"Are you doing some matchmaking here?"

She lowers her voice. "Maybe. I remember how it went down back in high school, and he wasn't exactly a ball of sunshine after breaking up with her. He ended it on the day she decided to go to Columbia, spring of our senior year. It's a top school. Anyway, she was pissed because it's in the city, close enough he could've visited, but instead he cut ties."

"Huh."

She continues. "And get this, she was only at Columbia for a semester before her dad lost his job. Her parents couldn't afford the tuition, so she had to come home and transfer to the state university as a commuter. By that time, Max was involved with someone else, so she just wrote him off. I think it's only because she's looking for Mr. Right that she got so irritated to see him cruising for a date in front of her. Probably didn't help that she'd had two margaritas. She wasn't holding back on speaking her mind."

I blink, surprised at how much she shared. "It must've been serious if they're still yelling at each other more than ten years later."

"Exactly," she says. "To be perfectly honest, she's been hung up on Drew forever, and it's a complete—hey, *you*!"

Audrey just opened the door. "Hey, you two ready to go? I'm locking up."

"Of course." Jenna maneuvers out of her seat, hopping a bit. I hand her crutches to her.

The two of them walk out together, and I follow. I'm not sure if I should invite Max to ladies' night. What if it makes Audrey angry?

I say bye to them and go to my car. Better not to get in the middle of that mess. Max is on his own where Audrey's concerned. He doesn't share about his women with me. We just play video games or watch horror movies. He's never with a woman long enough to interrupt our hang time for long.

I start my car and blast the heat. It takes forever for the car to get warm on a cold winter night. I drive off, my fingers gripping the steering wheel tight. So I have some baggage around modeling. I'll just think about that Boston terrier with a bowtie needing a home or the mother-daughter cat pair, and everything will be fine. Right? I have two days to psych myself up for it.

I break out in a sweat despite the cold of the car. *For the animals, for the animals...*

10

The next day I'm at ladies' night again, or what Sydney and friends call Thursday Night Wine Club. I can't help but notice not one of them is drinking wine. A former book club that never read books turned into a wine club that never drinks wine. Irony.

I'm still a little surprised at how easily this group of woman has included me. Sydney, Jenna, and Audrey go way back. Kayla's the newcomer this past year and now me. I'm on the end of the group next to Kayla. By my second beer, I'm actually laughing along with them, feeling comfortable. Sydney just shared a funny story about her husband, Wyatt, fussing over their dog Snowball, a white shih tzu. She says Wyatt struggles three times a day to keep little fuzzy boots on Snowball's paws for their walks. She showed us a picture of the boots on a disgruntled-looking Snowball. The boots are tiny gray things with lamb's wool inside. Apparently, Snowball's more interested in chewing them than walking in them.

Kayla leans against my shoulder. "So-o-o how's things with Caleb?"

The other women are still talking about dog snow boots because Jenna thinks they're a great idea for her dogs. I meet Kayla's kind brown eyes and find myself confiding in her. "I'm a little overwhelmed. He brought up marriage on our first date. He comes on really strong, talking about a thunderbolt when we first connected. I mean, does that sound normal?"

"Ooh, I don't know enough about his dating history to know." She digs her phone out of her purse. "Let me check in with Adam to see what's up." Alarm fires through me. Adam is Caleb's older brother and Kayla's fiancé. This will definitely get back to Caleb.

"No, wait. Just between us, okay?"

She puts her phone back. "Got it. Girl code."

"What's that?"

"You know, when you talk about your guy with your girl friends. Girl code says our lips are sealed. I way overshared about Adam when we were still on shaky ground. Sometimes you just need your friends' perspective on things."

"Cool."

Sydney looks over from Kayla's other side. "I hate to interrupt since you're girl coding over there, but I heard thunderbolt. I think I can be of help here." Sydney is Caleb's older sister. I guess I'll have to leave The Horseman Inn if I want to avoid running into people connected to him. This *is* a Robinson family establishment. His oldest brother, Drew, is in the far corner, watching the game on the TV. Pretty sure he can't hear from over there. Still.

"Girl code," I whisper.

Sydney socks my shoulder. "Absolutely. I'm sharing for your benefit. So, Dad always talked about the first time he met Mom as feeling like he was struck by a thunderbolt. Bam! He knew right then she was the one he'd marry. He even proposed on their first date. Of course she thought he was crazy, but after a month of dating and two more proposals, she finally agreed. They married, had the five of us, and lived very happily together. So Caleb told you he felt a thunderbolt for you?"

I stare at the bar top. "Oh, wow," I mutter. I saw those happy family pictures at his place. I know how much his family means to him, so does that mean he just really wants to believe the thunderbolt happened for him like his dad? No other guy has ever fallen instantly for me, especially a guy like him who could have anyone.

"Sloane?" Sydney prompts.

I turn to her. "That's what he said. Thunderbolt." I leave out the part where he said we can't have sex until I agree to marry him. His sister doesn't need to know about our sex life, or lack thereof. Though there was that one naked time...

"She's overwhelmed," Kayla puts in.

Sydney smiles. "I'm sure my mom felt the same. Give him a month. See what happens."

"A month," I echo.

Sydney nods once. "If it's really the thunderbolt, that's all it'll take to seal the deal. Of course it depends on how you feel about marriage."

"And him," Kayla says.

"How do you feel about him?" Sydney asks.

I notice Jenna and Audrey are leaning in, listening with rapt attention.

I swallow hard, not used to sharing intimacies with a group of women. Guys never talk about feelings stuff like this. "I like him, but—"

"It's a start," Sydney says, looking pleased. "You think you might like a serious relationship?"

"Like marriage?" My voice cracks. I have nothing against marriage to the right person. It's just a bit much to talk about it so soon.

Her light brown eyes are sympathetic. "Don't feel like you have to rush on that. Caleb's probably overly enthusiastic because he believes it happened for him just like Dad. But I will say this." She lifts a finger in the air. "Caleb has never shown any interest in marriage before this. Women chase him, and he can take or leave them. Nothing lasts long, and it never bothers him."

"He chased me!" I exclaim.

She grins. "That might be part of your appeal."

"That's what I was worried about. He's into the chase, and then once he catches me..." I trail off, remembering how I brought that up, and that was when he said no sex until marriage. He said he wasn't playing around.

"Once he catches you, he'll dump you?" Kayla asks.

She's very perceptive. I relax. It makes it easier to share when someone understands what I'm struggling with. "Yeah. Like if I let down my defenses, he'll just rip my heart out and walk away, losing all interest."

"Oh no, Caleb isn't like that," Kayla says. "He's the sweetest of the Robinsons. I think it's because he's the youngest. No offense, Sydney."

"I never aspired to be sweet," Sydney says, tossing back her whiskey. "I kick ass. You're the sweetest in your family, though, Kayla."

I stifle a laugh. Sydney's also saying her husband, Wyatt, isn't sweet. Kayla is not only engaged to Sydney's brother, Adam, she's also Wyatt's sister. I've only met Wyatt once when he was working behind the bar with Betsy, sharing about the drinks he served up, which he does for free because he's a whiskey and beer afficionado and helped Sydney select the inventory. He seemed like a confident cheerful guy.

Kayla beams and turns to me. "It's true, I'm the sweetest. I'm also the youngest like Caleb. In my family, Wyatt is brash, Paige is tough as nails, and Brooke is jaded, mostly to hide a mushy center. I guess Caleb and I are sweet because we're the youngest and were so well cared for by our older siblings. I know I was lucky in that regard. I had Wyatt watching over me and always knew Paige and Brooke were in my corner."

Sydney sighs. "I'll admit I babied Caleb. He was only eight when Mom died. I showered him with all my love and let him get away with a lot too. Dad was busy working here and missed some of what went on at home."

"There's nothing wrong with showering him with love," Kayla declares. "In fact, I bet that's why he's so cheerful. Adam says nothing gets Caleb down. He's perpetually sunny, even first thing in the morning."

"I can't take all the credit," Sydney says. "He was even a cheerful baby. Probably why he's always been popular too. People love Caleb; the camera loves Caleb…"

They both turn to me like I'm supposed to fill in the rest of that sentence.

I lift my palms. "We've had two dates."

"Third time's the charm," Sydney says with a grin.

Caleb

I walk into the open studio space in a Manhattan loft with Sloane, part of me hoping to impress her. As soon as I shut the door behind us, I unhook Huckleberry's leash and let him go on his sniffing tour. Rock music blares from a portable speaker. The loft with exposed brick and gleaming hardwood floors is empty except for the photographer's setup with a large white backdrop, lights, camera on a tripod, and a few metal folding chairs. I'm glad to see Dmitri got here early. He's adjusting the blinds on the wall of windows at the far end of the space. The models aren't here yet, but it's fifteen minutes until call time, so I'm not too worried.

I set down a bag with plastic water bowls for the dogs, paper towels, cleaner, and doggy bags in case of accidents. Then I take Sloane's hand, approaching Dmitri. He's in his forties, dressed casually in an untucked white button-down shirt, faded jeans, and loafers. His dark hair is cut even shorter than mine. "Nice space you found," I call over the music.

He turns, his brows lifting. "As long as the sun cooperates." He pulls his phone out, lowers the volume on the music, and strides over to greet us, stopping short in front of Sloane, his hands forming a frame around her face. "Look at those eyes. Like cat eyes, a golden amber. Magnificent. Can I get your picture?"

Sloane backs up a step. "I'm just here to help with the dogs."

He smiles. "Sorry, first things first. I'm Dmitri Gulko." He offers his hand.

She gives his hand a shake. "Sloane."

He glances at me. "So striking with the dark hair and golden eyes."

"Isn't she?"

Sloane's rosy cheeks redden, and she mutters something about light brown eyes.

"How about a picture of the two of you together?" he asks, raising his brows at me. He's gotten plenty of pictures of me in the past. He really wants Sloane.

"That's okay," Sloane says, letting go of my hand to walk to the far windows.

Dmitri speaks under his breath. "She has no idea of her beauty. What a unique look, and somehow the baggy sweater and ripped jeans work on that petite frame. Effortlessly chic."

Fact is, the baggy sweater slides off one shoulder, exposing her delicate collarbone and shoulder, and the jeans are formfitting. So sexy. "I thought so too. Even more cool, she's a mechanic."

He stares at her. "I need to take her picture at work. Do you know how many car afficionados would buy *anything* with her in the ad?" Dmitri does a lot of ad work.

"She's shy." I know she said she wasn't, but I don't quite believe her. She's slow to warm up, not very talkative, and she blushes easily. "Best to lay off the photo thing. It makes her uncomfortable."

"Shame," he says.

The door opens, and Gerard, a tall guy with dark hair, piercing blue eyes, and huge muscles, walks in holding a miniature white poodle tucked in the crook of his arm. "Bonnie and I are ready for our closeup. Can we be February? She looks good against pink and red backgrounds. You know, for Valentine's Day."

Huckleberry races over, barking. I give him the sit command and walk over, holding him by the collar, giving Bonnie a chance to get comfortable.

"February's all yours," I say, giving Bonnie a pet. "Appreciate you doing this."

"Anything for you. We came up together with those fitness supplement ads."

He sets Bonnie down, and Huckleberry leaps to his feet. Sloane rushes over to Bonnie, probably to protect her, but Bonnie freaks, turns, and runs. That inspires Huckleberry to chase. Gerard races after Bonnie at the same time as Sloane.

"Sloane, grab Huckleberry's collar," I call.

She changes direction just as Gerard pivots, and they slam into each other. His arms go around her, halting her fall.

"Hello," he says warmly, looking down at her.

"Sorry," she says, stepping out of his arms and smoothing her hair down.

I snap on Huckleberry's leash, and Gerard scoops up Bonnie again. "Is she with anyone?" Gerard whispers to me.

"Me," I say. "Don't even think about it."

Sloane walks over and takes Huckleberry's leash. "Sorry. I'll keep him on leash with me. Let's introduce them to each other. Huckleberry, sit." She waits for him to sit, and then she says, "This is Bonnie. We don't chase her, but you can sniff."

Gerard obligingly leans down, letting Huckleberry sniff Bonnie. Bonnie stays perfectly still, her little nose quivering. Huckleberry finishes his perusal with a lick on her nose.

"Okay, now we're all friends," Sloane says.

I introduce her to Gerard, who gives her his smoldering smile. "Nice to meet you, Sloane."

"Likewise," she says without even a hint of a blush. That means his smolder didn't work. Ha. "You have a leash for her? I'll keep them both at my side. Caleb, where's the toys?"

"Crap. I left them in the trunk of my car. I'll go get them."

I race out the door, leaving Sloane to two men who see her like I do—a cool, effortlessly beautiful woman. The fact that she doesn't know it only adds to her appeal. I've never met another woman like her.

It takes me a good fifteen minutes to get to where I parked in a nearby garage, get the toy box, and get back.

I step inside, expecting a full house with eleven models and their dogs, but it's just Gerard and two other model friends, Rusty and Shane. Including me, we only have four models for a calendar. That's not going to work. It's supposed to be a new face and dog for every month.

I greet them and go over to Dmitri. "Let's just get started. Hopefully the others will show soon."

Only they don't. I call and text them, getting only voicemail and a few lame excuses that a paying gig came up. It's for charity, and they agreed to donate their time. I'm pissed and feel like I wasted the rental space and Dmitri's time, who did this as a favor to me. Dammit.

I go last so the other models can leave when they're done their turn. Sloane had an easy time of it with the dogs. Huckleberry was the only big dog. The others—a Yorkie, miniature poodle, and greyhound—spent most of their time napping in a warm corner on the greyhound's bed. Huckleberry stuck close to Sloane.

Now it's my turn. Just me, Sloane, and Dmitri are left.

"Hang onto Huckleberry for a minute," I tell her.

She holds up his leash to show me she's been hanging onto him. She's sitting on the floor with her legs crisscrossed, Huckleberry lying next to her, his head resting on his paws as he keeps his eyes on me. I take my shirt off and set it over the back of a metal folding chair.

Sloane watches me with interest. Not like she's crazed with lust so much as she's curious about my modeling work.

Dmitri spritzes me with oil.

"Okay, release the hound," I call to Sloane.

She smiles and unclips his leash. "Go see Caleb." She has to give Huckleberry a nudge before he gets up, stretches his back legs and then his front legs.

"Come on, Huckleberry," I say, slapping my thigh.

He walks over, and I crouch down, praising him as I pet him. I hear the camera clicking away. It's not easy to pose with him. The smaller dogs can be lifted, not Huckleberry.

Sloane wanders over. "Try lying down, side by side with him."

"Yes," Dmitri says. "That's good."

I give Huckleberry the down command. As soon as he lies down, I get on my belly next to him. The camera snaps away as we look at each other up close, and then Dmitri snaps his fingers, and we both look at the camera.

"I'll have him run through his tricks," I say. Then I give him commands while I work around him. He sits, we shake paws, and he rolls over. I rub his belly for that, and he wiggles on his back, which makes me laugh.

"Lots of fun pics," Dmitri says. "Let's get you both upright and go for a sexy smolder. Pretend the camera is your beauty Sloane here."

Sloane watches intently as I do my thing, loving the camera.

Once Dmitri is satisfied, he turns to Sloane. "Sure you don't want a picture of the two of you?"

She shakes her head. "No, thanks. You've done enough work today."

"Not work. It would be my pleasure."

She looks down at her outfit. "I'm not dressed for a picture."

Dmitri gestures toward me. "He's shirtless. I think your sweater is perfect. If you just tuck it in here." He gestures to the front of his jeans.

She tucks it in. Guess she's okay with it.

"Scoot over, Huckleberry," I say, nudging him to the right. He's sprawled in the center of the backdrop now, relaxing.

I crook my finger at Sloane.

She walks over and turns to Dmitri. "This is just a souvenir picture for us. I don't want this in the calendar or online anywhere, okay?"

"Absolutely," he says. "Stand facing each other."

I band an arm around her waist and bring her close, a familiar jolt going through me when her amber eyes meet mine. Her cheeks flush as she looks up at me, her lips parting. The camera clicks away.

"The contrast in your coloring and size makes such a tableau," Dmitri says. "Caleb, wrap your arms around her from behind."

I turn her and settle my hands on her hips and then wrap them around her waist, leaning down to smile at her.

"He's taking so many pictures," she whispers.

"That's his thing. He'll let us pick our favorite later."

We both turn our heads, looking at the camera.

"Sloane, you're a natural!" Dmitri exclaims. "Have you done modeling before?"

Silence.

I lean forward to look at her. Her lips are pressed tightly together. "Sloane?" I prompt.

She pulls away. "That's plenty of pictures."

Dmitri lowers his camera. "You want to see?" He offers her a peek at the back of his digital camera.

"Later, thanks." She walks off to get Huckleberry's leash.

Dmitri and I exchange a puzzled look. He was just complimenting her, but it seemed to make her shut down.

He packs up his stuff while Sloane and I clean up the space, gathering toys and cleaning spilled water from the dogs' bowls.

"Have a good weekend!" Dmitri calls. "Nice to meet you, Sloane."

"Thanks, you too," Sloane says.

"Dmitri, thanks for everything," I say. "I owe you."

He smiles. "Always happy to help a good cause."

Once he leaves, Sloane says, "It's so lame the other models didn't show up today. Sorry."

I blow out a breath. "Yeah."

"What're you going to do?"

"I don't know. I guess just work with what we have, even though it's not as appealing to reuse the same model for multiple months. Dmitri got enough pictures in different poses I could do it."

She shakes her head. "Get local guys to fill in the other months. Your brothers and any other young guy. I could get Max, oh, and the vet in town, Dr. Russo. I saw him on his website, and he's not bad to look at. Even our mayor could get in on it. Lots of women are into the bearded look Levi's got going on." She counts on her fingers. "That's six guys right there. Then we only need two more. I could ask Max if someone from his landscape crew would be willing to pose."

I scowl, mostly because it's clear she's close with Max, and I hate that I'm so territorial about her. Normally I'm very laid-back with women. "That won't work. Let's go." I grab Huckleberry's leash and head out the door.

Sloane keeps up by my side. "Why not?"

I lock the door behind us and find myself admitting the truth. "Because those people aren't models, and they'll think it's dumb." *They'll think I'm dumb.*

"It's not dumb. It's for a good cause. I'm sure Dr. Russo would be all for it since it's for his shelter. And I know I can convince Max. All I have to do is promise him pizza's on me for the next month."

I walk to the elevator and punch the button. I keep my mouth shut so I won't sound like a jealous boyfriend. I'm not even sure I am her boyfriend. She only agreed to come here today because Jenna asked her. She turned me down when I asked.

We step inside the elevator while I try to cool my temper. I'm just frustrated and unsure where I stand with her. A completely new experience for me.

Sloane looks thoughtful. "Actually, I'd be out two months' worth of pizza. I already promised him a month's worth to help me organize the royal ball for Winterfest."

That's it. Max is definitely into her. What guy wants to organize a ball? "What royal ball?"

She explains about Audrey researching other winter festivals and how she thought it would be a good idea to adopt the idea of a king and queen for our Winterfest. Hmm, maybe Max agreed to work more closely with Audrey. I can't assume that's why, though. It's just as likely for Sloane.

"If it was Audrey's idea, why isn't she working on that?" I ask.

"She's already in charge of programs, ticket sales, and advertising for Winterfest."

"I'm joining this committee. I'll help you plan the ball and whatever else you need."

Her face lights up. "Really? Oh, thank you so much. I'm in way over my head. I never even went to a dance before, let alone planned a fancy event. And the coronation is, like, blowing my mind. I don't have a clue how that's supposed to go. I put Max in charge of researching what to do."

Yeah, I definitely need to be there.

"Wait, you never went to a dance?" I ask. "Not even prom?"

She crouches down to pet Huckleberry. "Those things are lame anyway. Right, Huckleberry?"

I read between the lines. No one asked her to go. Idiots.

The elevator opens on the ground floor, and I let her go out with Huckleberry first. As soon as we step into the hallway, I inform her, "We'll go to the ball together."

"It's five weeks away."

"So?"

She shakes her head. "Nothing."

She doesn't believe we're going to last. For some reason, she still doesn't seem to get how into her I am. It's time I show her a good time, here in the city.

I tip her chin up and kiss her. "You'll be my queen."

She blinks a few times. "I guess that makes you my king?"

"You'll get used to it."

"Did anyone ever tell you that you're delusional?"

I grab her and dip her over my arm. She yelps, which makes Huckleberry bark excitedly.

"Caleb!" Her amber eyes are bright. She looks happy. I pull her upright and give her a quick kiss. "Let's go, my queen."

She laughs, and we walk out of the building hand in hand, Huckleberry trotting beside us.

11

Sloane

I go back to Caleb's apartment in Gramercy Park. It's a rent-controlled two-bedroom, which is rare, held under the agency's owner's name. The great thing about Caleb is that, even though he was upset the modeling shoot didn't go like he hoped, he didn't let that ruin our time together. He even volunteered to help me with Winterfest.

He called me his queen. And damn if I don't feel kinda special now.

"Looks like Hugo is here," Caleb says, indicating a black down jacket on a hook by the door. Water runs in the bathroom. Caleb walks down the hall toward the bedrooms and returns. "He put his suitcases in the right room. I need to make sure he's situated and knows what's what. He's twenty and just flew in from Sweden. This is his first trip to New York. You want a bottled water?"

"Sure."

I sit on the sofa and watch Huckleberry do his tour of sniffing. That seems to be his thing when he arrives someplace new. Caleb's place is sparse. There's a dark green sofa, coffee table, and TV in the living room open to a small dining area and, behind a half wall, a galley kitchen. The two bedrooms and bathroom are down a short hallway from the living room. The nice thing is, the living room has three windows with views of the city.

I wander over to the windows, looking at the buildings and the fenced-in park in the distance.

"Hey, man, I'm Caleb, your roommate."

Huckleberry barks and runs over to a stunning tall guy with thick blond shoulder-length hair, still wet from the shower, ice blue eyes, and high cheekbones. Hugo looks like a Norse god. He's wearing a beige Henley shirt with jeans and sneakers.

"Nice to meet you," Hugo says, shaking Caleb's hand and then giving Huckleberry a quick pat.

"This is my girlfriend, Sloane," Caleb says, indicating me.

My pulse kicks up, warmth spreading through me. I guess it's official. I'm his girlfriend. Well, he did say I was his queen, so I guess the girlfriend part was implied.

Hugo walks over to me, Huckleberry following him to sniff his jeans. "I'm Hugo. Nice to meet you too." He offers his hand.

I place my hand in his, and he gives it a firm shake.

"This is a very nice apartment," Hugo says to Caleb. "Everyone says New York City has tiny apartments with cockroaches and rats. Not so." There's a musicality to his voice that's fun to hear, and his English is impressive.

"How did you learn English so well?" I ask.

Hugo laughs. "Lots of people in Sweden speak English. We're taught in school, and I watch English programs on TV. I also went to summer camp in the US for three summers in Vermont. Beautiful place, lots of girls to practice my English on." He flashes a wicked smile.

"I bet," Caleb says with a laugh. "Did you check in with the agency already?"

"Yes. I've got my US phone and changed money to US dollars."

"Great. So let me show you where stuff is, give you the lay of the land, and then we'll grab some dinner."

"I want to go to a club tonight," Hugo says. "I've heard they get really wild here."

Caleb claps a hand on his back. "Got news for you, bud. Those clubs are twenty-one and older."

"We can get fake ID, yeah?"

"No, we do nothing shady. Ever. But don't worry, there's plenty of parties I can take you to." He guides him into the kitchen, pointing out where stuff is, the take-out menus, and also everything he needs to make green smoothies. I find myself smiling, listening to Caleb launch into a lecture on taking care of yourself and how important it is, not just for looking good on camera, but for staying healthy.

"Steer clear of alcohol the night before a photo shoot," Caleb warns. "It'll show in your face. Puffy eyes and cheeks. No good."

Hugo inclines his head, his hair sweeping over one eye. "In Sweden, the drinking age is eighteen. No big deal. Twenty-one is very late."

"You'll see plenty of alcohol at parties. Everything in moderation and that includes partying. It's eat healthy, exercise, and sleep. If you can't do all three for whatever reason, pick two. I can't emphasize this enough. The key to a successful modeling career depends on you taking good care of yourself. I'll be here until Sunday night. I'll hook you up with a green smoothie tomorrow morning, get you off to a good start."

"Is this mandatory?" Hugo asks.

"Yes, Hugo, it is."

Hugo turns to me. "Does he make you drink green smoothies?"

"I've never had breakfast with him. We just started seeing each other."

"You want to spend the night?" Caleb asks me. "That's a sofa bed there." He points to the green sofa. "I can see what's going on tonight. There's always a party somewhere on Friday night."

Hugo chuckles. "You make your girlfriend sleep on a sofa bed? Maybe I have a thing or two to teach you."

"Mind your business," Caleb says, smiling. He pulls his phone from his pocket. "See? Just got an invite from a music producer I did a video with a few months back. Usually Tigran's penthouse is packed with rock stars and models. Sound good?"

"Yeah!" Hugo cheers. "Wicked cool." His slang must be from his summer camp. People up in the New England area say wicked.

Caleb turns to me. "You in, my queen?"

How can I say no? He called me a queen.

"I have to be back in Summerdale by noon tomorrow," I say. "I have tutoring at the library."

"I didn't know you tutored."

"Yeah, I have a couple of kids I'm tutoring in math right now. One's in fifth grade, the other tenth."

He gazes into my eyes, his lips curving up. "Cool. We'll pick up whatever toiletries you need on our way home from dinner. You hungry?"

"Yeah."

"How about you, Hugo?"

Hugo shakes his head. "I don't want to intrude on your date with your queen."

Caleb laughs. "Room for all in the royal court. C'mon, dinner's on me."

Hugo turns to me. "Are you sure it's okay?"

"Absolutely. Besides, I'm sure Caleb wants to make sure you're eating a healthy dinner."

Caleb inclines his head toward the door. "Let's go. And, Hugo, stay away from the hot dog carts."

"I thought I was getting a roommate not a babysitter," Hugo grumbles.

Caleb stops short. "I look out for the new guy. The agency doesn't pay me to do that. I do it because I want you to succeed. Got it?" He offers Hugo a fist bump.

He returns the fist bump. "Got it."

"You'll see I can be a lot of fun."

I smile at Hugo. "He did name his dog Huckleberry."

"That's a silly name for a dog like this," Hugo says. "He should be named Koda or Zeus."

I smile. "Right?"

Hugo and I walk out the door together, coming up with lots of dignified names for Huckleberry. Caleb has a brief scuffle at the door, getting Huckleberry to stay behind in the apartment, before joining us and dropping an arm around my shoulders as we walk.

My cheeks flush, but I play it cool like we always walk like this. Like we're a real couple. Maybe by the end of this weekend, I'll feel like we really are.

∿

I may not be cool enough for this party, even with my upgrade from sneakers to black platform boots with a block heel. Caleb bought them for me at a shop we passed after dinner, and I frigging love them. They're badass and give me an inch in height without making me wobble. We're at a two-level penthouse apartment owned by Tigran, a music producer. The whole place is done in white with just a few pops of black for contrast in the overhead lighting and a couple of modern angular leather and chrome chairs. This is not a home you could have kids, dogs, or red wine. At least I couldn't. I'd be forever worried about staining the white.

We've been here for an hour. Hugo disappeared almost immediately, placing himself in the center of a group of women, who took to him right away, fawning over his accent.

I've never met more rock stars or seen so many glossy women before. Caleb is in his element, talking and laughing with everyone. I slip away to use the restroom. This party reminds me of when I first met Caleb at The Horseman Inn during his family's engagement celebration. I'm on the outside of a group that adores him. He's the sun that everyone revolves around. I'm not even one of those planets rotating around him. I'm in his shadow, unnoticed, disappearing into the background.

I knock on the bathroom door on the lower level.

"Someone's in here!" a woman's voice calls.

I wait, fiddling with the bottom of my sweater. I'm so underdressed for this party. The women are wearing tight dresses, short skirts, and a few are in pants suits. Everyone looks like they just stepped off the runway. Whatever. I wouldn't feel comfortable dressed like that anyway.

The door pops open, and a tall red-haired woman in a silver jumpsuit that's open to her navel narrows her eyes at me. Caleb introduced us earlier. Rochelle. He worked with her on the Cali Pop campaign.

"Hi," I say.

She looks down at me with a condescending sneer. "Are you really with Caleb?"

"Excuse me?"

"You're so—" she gestures vaguely in the air "—*ordinary*. Be honest, are you his assistant? He brought you here to get the lay of the land, right?"

I press my lips together. "I'm a mechanic. How's that for ordinary?" I stand out whether I like it or not.

She lifts her perfectly arched brows. "That's weird."

"You're weird."

She scoffs. "Honey, you are *way* out of your league. You'll never keep him." She stalks off on stilettos.

My eyes and cheeks are hot as I step into the bathroom. The tile is glaringly white. My body goes numb, moving on autopilot.

I catch a glimpse of myself in the mirror when I wash my hands. My face is pale, my eyes shiny with unshed tears. *Don't let her get in your head. She's jealous. She probably wants Caleb.*

I let myself out, and the sound of high female laughter reaches me. I hesitate. I'm not ready to join Caleb in the center of it all again, surrounded by his glamorous admirers.

I find the kitchen, separate from the main living space, where the caterer is frying up some kind of dumpling. She's an older woman, her black and gray hair in a neat bun, wearing a white apron over a long-sleeve black shirt and turquoise floral skirt.

"It smells delicious," I say.

She smiles and nods.

"A lot of people here. You must be working hard."

She nods and turns a dumpling onto a platter lined with paper towels.

"Pretty glam," I say, pulling out a chair across the island from where she's cooking. "It's nice to get a little quiet."

She smiles and nods.

For the first time since I got here, I finally relax. It's nice to have someone who's so good at listening. I tell her about Caleb and Hugo and the cool place we had dinner earlier with fairy lights, an old jukebox, and super friendly waiters. Food was good too. Then I confide what I typically do for work and how that makes me feel so-o-o out of place here. I don't spill the mean things Rochelle said, but it feels good to get that much off my chest.

I stick around for a while, eating dumplings with these delicious sauces she prepares. I'm lucky I got first crack at the caterer's food. Who knows how long it would take this stuff to make its way to me out there with all those people?

Caleb pokes his head in. "There you are."

"Hi, I was just getting a snack. She's a fantastic cook." I realize I didn't catch her name. "Sorry, here I've been blabbing all this time, and I never introduced myself. I'm Sloane."

Caleb gives her a small wave and a smile. "Bye."

"But—" He pulls me right out of my chair. I'm so surprised I don't say a word. He pulls me down a narrow hallway and into the bathroom, shutting and locking the door. "What're you doing?"

"What are *you* doing?" he returns in a fierce whisper. "I take you to a party full of rock stars, and you hide in the kitchen?"

"I wasn't hiding. I was just chatting with the caterer." I lift my chin. "She's no less important because of her job than a musician."

He narrows his eyes. "That's Tigran's mom. She's Armenian and doesn't speak a word of English, so I'm not exactly sure how you were chatting with her."

I open my mouth and then shut it. I thought she was just a good listener. She smiled and nodded a lot and occasionally said, "Ah."

"Everyone needs company," I say defensively. "She was all by herself, and you didn't need me. You had a group of admirers."

"Are you really that shy?" Caleb asks.

"I told you I'm not shy."

"Right. Okay. Well, parties like these aren't just about having a good time. This is how I get jobs, social networking. Tigran knows everyone. Music videos are legit work for models, and it pays well, but instead of talking to people, I'm on a wild-goose chase looking for you. I thought you left."

I cross my arms, looking to the side. "I wouldn't just leave. I mean, where would I go?"

"You could take a train home."

I hadn't even considered that, but the idea cheers me up instantly. This world just isn't for me. It was probably a good thing I was forced out of the industry when I was a kid, no matter how much it hurt at the time. But Caleb shines here. Everyone loves him, he loves everyone right back, and he's a positive influence on the younger models. His hometown mechanic girlfriend is the odd duck. What else is new? But at least back home I'm comfortable.

I take a deep breath and lay it on the line. "I'm sorry, this just isn't my thing. I thought it would be cool, and it was at first, but then I just felt really uncomfortable and out of place. You probably didn't notice, but some of your female groupies are giving me side-eye. They want you all to themselves, and I'm in the way."

He looks to the ceiling before leveling me with a hard look. "If I wanted anyone at this party, I wouldn't have brought you. You get that, right? I thought we were on the same page here. We're a thing."

"But that doesn't mean I fit in your life. These are your people."

He spreads his hands wide. "Everyone is my people. I like everyone."

Caleb attracts people because he makes everyone feel special. It shouldn't take away from how special I felt when he said I was his queen, but it does. I blink rapidly, my throat tight. I don't know why I'm getting so emotional. I always knew we didn't fit together.

"Can we go back to the party now?" he asks.

"I can't do this," I say quietly.

"Do what?"

I gesture wildly. "This. The glam party scene. I'm an imposter here. I don't fit, and maybe that means I don't fit in your life either."

12

The words hang in the air between us. My heart pounds as he stares at me. I don't want to end things with Caleb, but it's so obvious we don't fit.

"Don't you see how our two worlds don't go together?" I ask softly. "You're in this glamorous modeling world, and I'm wearing coveralls covered in motor oil." I swallow hard. "And you just recently got a major campaign with more on the horizon. Next thing you know, you'll be full-time jet-setting around the world."

He takes a deep breath. "Sloane, as long as we work, nothing else matters."

I speak over the lump in my throat. "Of course it matters. I don't fit."

"But you could," he says. "If you could just get to a point where you're comfortable—"

"I'm never gonna be comfortable! I've been burned by these people!"

His eyes widen. "You're really upset. Okay, we're going now."

He opens the door and guides me out. After a quick goodbye to our host and a few other people who grab Caleb's arm on the way out, we make it outside. The cold night air hits me, and I feel like I can breathe again.

He hails a cab, and we head back to his apartment in silence. I'm tempted to call it a night, but I owe him an explanation for blowing up at him back there. And disappointing him. My heart feels heavy. I just know once I explain myself, he's going to see as clearly as I do that we simply don't fit together. Never mind the thunderbolt, as romantic as that sounded.

Once inside his apartment, he takes care of Huckleberry, taking him out for a quick walk. A few minutes later, Caleb's orchestrated a very relaxing setup. We left our shoes by the door, and now we're settled on the sofa with glasses of white wine. I have a feeling this is his seduction routine. Soft music plays in the background, and he even dimmed the lights. Huckleberry is sleeping on the floor under the small square dining table.

"When's Hugo getting back?" I ask.

"I imagine late," he says. "Okay, explain what you meant before. You said you've been burned by these people. What people do you mean? You didn't know anyone there, so how could they have burned you?"

Damn, it's not a seduction. He was getting me nice and relaxed so I'll spill my guts.

I stare at the floor. "That woman Rochelle you worked with for Cali Pop, she, uh, said I was ordinary and also weird and that I'll never be able to keep you."

He mutters a curse and pulls me close. "Don't listen to her. You're extraordinary. She's jealous of you."

I pull away. "If she's jealous, it's only because she wants you."

"I'll talk to her. That's not right the way she treated you." He shakes his head. "She seemed cool on our shoot. I hate that she made you feel bad."

I take a long swallow of wine. "It's not just her. I meant it when I said I don't fit in this world. With industry people. Beautiful people."

"I don't understand."

I stare straight ahead. "When I was very little, Mom started entering me in kiddy beauty pageants."

"How little?"

"Three." I take another sip of wine. "She was…it was like our thing. We were very connected over competing on the pageant circuit, and then when I was six, I won a major contest and got an agent. So from age six to eleven, I was a child model and did a few commercials too. I, uh, never grew tall, so modeling as an adult was out."

"That's it? You're too short is the reason you feel so uncomfortable around industry people? I thought someone treated you badly."

I drain my wine and set the glass on the coffee table. "Here's more truth for you. I hit an awkward stage, and a photographer told Mom that she should forget booking me more work because I was the opposite of the ugly duckling. Started out—" my voice chokes "—adorable and then not."

"What an asshole. Sloane—"

I hold up a hand. "There's more. It wasn't just the end of my career with a shame-inducing spiral right when I was at the height of self-consciousness. The worst part is I lost the bonding thing with Mom. She was so disappointed in me she left. She said I was the only reason she'd stuck around as long as she had. I guess when I was no longer a cute kid, she had no use for me."

He sets his glass down and pulls me close, wrapping an arm around my shoulders. "I'm so sorry you went through all that. She missed out by not seeing you grow into the amazing woman you are today."

I lean my cheek against his solid warm chest. "It's okay. I'm fine." I'm dry-eyed, all out of tears over the past. Still, I don't pull away. "I guess you see why I don't feel good in your modeling world. I have some kind of post-traumatic stress over it."

He strokes my hair. "Of course you do. Double whammy with your career ending and your mom leaving. I don't know anything about your mom, but usually divorce happens when the relationship goes sour. I'm sure it wasn't because of you she left."

I sit up. "Obviously she wasn't close with my dad. They

only married because she was pregnant with me. She stayed when I was useful and left when I wasn't."

"That's her loss and not your fault. You get that, right?"

"Cause-effect. I both started and ended the marriage. Seems pretty straightforward to me."

"You were a kid. You can't take that on yourself. She was an adult and made some bad decisions."

I run my fingers along the edge of the sofa, not convinced. "I'm sure everyone at that party wondered what you were doing with me. We're like beauty and the beast in reverse. You being the epitome of male beauty."

"Don't talk about yourself like that."

I shrug. "I'm no one's ideal woman. It's not a secret or anything."

He scowls and then pulls out his phone. "Look at this." He taps a few times and pulls up an album of photos. "Dmitri sent these over from earlier today. He didn't have time for editing or retouching. These are the originals. Look at you. You're beautiful."

My lips crook to the side, disbelieving. I look. My cheeks have a rosy pink to them. My eyes and skin seem to glow. The way I'm looking at Caleb, and the way he's looking at me, we look like a couple in love.

I turn to him, the truth slowly sinking in. "We actually look natural together."

He leans his cheek against mine as we scroll through the photos. "You look like you're really into me," he murmurs.

"I was going to say the same thing about you."

We face each other, gazing into each other's eyes.

"I'm sorry I ruined the party for you tonight," I say.

"You see now that no one would ever question why I'm with you, right?" He tucks a lock of hair behind my ear, his fingers grazing my neck. "We look like we're—"

"In love," I breathe.

He smiles widely. "I was going to say a couple, but I like your version better."

I throw my arms around his neck and kiss him passion- ately. He returns the kiss with equal heat. His hands roam all over me as we kiss like there's nothing more important in the world. *Never stop.* Lips and tongue and teeth. I need it all. Every sensation.

Caleb scoops me off the sofa and carries me to his bedroom. He sets me on my feet next to the bed and kisses me again, his fingers spearing through my hair. We pull apart a breathless moment later. And then he strips me, slowly, kissing every inch of exposed skin. I sigh, my head dropping back. I've never had a guy take his time like this before.

He's kneeling, stripping off my socks. He kisses his way up my leg, dropping a kiss on my sex and then tasting. I stroke his hair, my breath stuttering out. He rises to his feet, and I grab his head, kissing him, my hands frantic to strip him too.

He breaks the kiss. "You sure about this?"

"Yes, absolutely," I say, high on the victory of removing his shirt. I immediately go for the button on his jeans, but he pushes my hands away, doing it himself. I see why when he carefully unzips over a massive bulge. He wants me as much as I want him. This is happening.

I grab him, kissing him, trying to climb him, eager to get as close as humanly possible. He picks me up easily and sets me in the center of the bed before joining me, covering me with his body. The sensation of skin on skin is exquisite.

He laces his fingers with mine and pins them to the mattress on either side of my head. His lips meet mine for a long, deep kiss. I'm so ready, so eager, and he's going so slow.

I tear my mouth away. "Caleb, I want you. Let's get this going."

He nips my lower lip and then licks it. "Our first time is meant to be savored. Lie back and relax."

"I—"

His kiss cuts me off, an all-consuming kiss that shows a hint of the same urgency I'm feeling. He's controlling himself, holding back. My hands are pinned under his, my body under his. I can't move this along. Something in me lets go. I relax under him, and his mouth becomes more demanding. Sensation rushes through me as I throb with need.

He shifts, kissing his way across my jaw, down my throat, across my collarbone, leaving a tingling trail. He releases my wrists as he kisses his way lower, finally reaching my breast, cupping it, and drawing the nipple into his mouth. He sucks, and intense desire fires through me. I hold him to me, breathing heavily, aching for him. He switches sides, lavishing attention on my other breast. *Oh God.* I'm already close. I never knew my breasts were so sensitive.

He pulls back, gazing at my breasts, and I'm suddenly self-conscious. I don't even need to wear a bra for support. It's for modesty's sake.

"I'm small," I say.

He looks up at me. "Everything about you is perfectly proportioned."

I smile, my eyes watering. "You too."

"Don't mind me," he murmurs, kissing his way down my stomach.

I hold my breath as he kisses along my inner thigh and keeps going, all the way to my toes. I reach for him.

His smoldering gaze gives me a jolt. He wants me badly, yet he's still taking his time. I can only assume it's because he cares about me, my pleasure. It's a whole new experience for me.

And then he spreads my legs wide, sliding them over his shoulders, and takes one long lick. I gasp, my hips jerking.

"Mmm," he hums against me.

I gasp again.

And then his mouth works magic. *Bliss.*

And his fingers join in. *Omigod.*

Suddenly I'm vibrating, coiled tight. *Please.*

And I break, my hips bucking wildly, the starburst of pleasure exploding deep within me. He keeps going, gentling his touch as I ride wave after wave until I'm spent, gasping for breath.

He reaches to the nightstand drawer. "Ready for more?"

I smile widely. He's so awesome. "Give it to me."

He rips open the packet and rolls the condom on. "You know what this means, right?"

"Fuck, yeah." It means I need him bad.

He kisses me, and I taste myself, an erotic sensation that makes me crazed. Then he's sliding inside, so thick I need to arch my hips to ease the way. He lifts his head, watching me as he finally fills me to the hilt.

My breath stutters out.

His fingers entwine with mine as he begins to move. Slow and deep, his gaze on mine. It's tender, almost soulful, and for the first time in my life, I know what making love means.

He shifts and hits a spot on the inside that makes me wild. I lift my hips, angling for more, and he gives it to me, driving home again and again. I shudder and then cry out, the orgasm ripping through me. He pounds into me, raw need driving him, and I take it, my breath coming in harsh pants with every jolt of pleasure.

His head arches back as he lets go with a guttural groan and then collapses on top of me. The breath whooshes from my lungs at his weight. I stroke his heated back, reveling in the hard planes.

He props up on his forearms and lifts his head. "Can you breathe? Sorry. I lost control at the end there."

I smile, a ridiculously goofy smile. "I'm fine. I love that you lost control."

He strokes my hair back, kisses me, and rolls to his side. We lie like that for a few minutes, catching our breath. I muster the energy to pull the covers over us and flop back down.

He plays with my hair. "Do you want to get married someday?"

"Yeah, someday."

"To me?"

I turn my head to meet his eyes. "I don't know. This is all so new."

"I'll wait until you know."

I prop up on an elbow to stare at him, baffled by his insistence on this thunderbolt that means we're destined for each other. It sounds more like family legend than reality. "Caleb, be practical. People don't just get hit by a thunderbolt and decide they're going to marry someone."

"How do you feel about kids?"

My mouth gapes.

"You must like them since you tutor them and you were a teacher."

I roll to my back, way out of my league with all this heavy talk.

He grabs me, and I shriek in surprise as he pulls me on top of him. His chest shakes with laughter. "Calm down, darling. I'm going to manhandle you sometimes. You're just the right size to make it work."

"You surprised me," I say in defense of my ridiculous high-pitched scream.

The heat of him is intoxicating. Every muscle in my body relaxes. His big hands massage over my shoulders and down my back. I melt into him.

His fingers trail up my spine to the nape of my neck, which he squeezes. "Tell me your secret fantasy."

The words are out without a thought. "A big happy family."

He stills under me, and then his hands push the hair out of my face as he shifts, trying to meet my eyes. I can feel his gaze.

I lift my head. "Silly fantasy of an only child."

His lips curve into a wide smile, his hazel eyes sparkling. "I meant sex fantasy, but that one is amazing. I can give you that. You can be part of my big happy family, and one day, if you want, we could have our own."

"Really?" I ask softly.

He kisses me. "Oh, Sloane, we're going to have it all."

And in that moment I feel like I already do.

"Be right back," he says, setting me back on the mattress. I watch him walk naked out to the hallway to the bathroom.

I stare at the ceiling, a little stunned. He said we wouldn't have sex until I agreed to marry him. Is that what I just agreed to? Part of me wants that, which is even crazier than believing in a thunderbolt. We've only been seeing each other for a week.

He returns, completely comfortable walking around naked, and slides under the covers, shifting me so he's spooning me from behind. I find I don't mind him maneuvering my body around. I always land in a nice position.

He strokes my hair back, his voice rumbling by my ear. "Tell me your dreams, anything big or small, and I'll make them happen." The man must be magic because I believe he's capable of anything.

"My dream is to be partner in Dad's shop."

"And if he refuses, what's your backup plan? Your dream shouldn't depend on someone else's cooperation."

"I never thought that far. I've just wanted to run it with him for as long as I can remember. A super mechanic team. There's no one better than him. I'm still learning from him."

"Okay, what else?"

"The big happy family," I admit. "I've never told anyone that before."

He cups my face and shifts me toward him for a kiss. "Beautiful."

I shift back, snuggling into him. His hand settles on my stomach, and I entwine my fingers with his. "What're your dreams?"

"My dreams are still fuzzy. I know I want a more settled career after modeling, but I haven't figured out what that is."

"That's okay. You don't have to know everything right this minute."

"True. What I've got going on right now is perfect."

I tense. His career is taking off, which means he'll leave me in the dust.

He kisses my neck. "I mean us."

I soften. "Oh, Caleb."

"You believe me about the thunderbolt now?"

"I'm starting to."

"Good because it's the truth."

"Now that we had sex, does that mean I have to marry you?"

He chuckles. "It means it's inevitable. Relax and enjoy the ride."

I smile to myself. This *is* the ride of my life.

As long as I don't think too hard on our differences, or the thunderbolt quickness of everything, as long as I don't think, period. Just feel. Right now, warm and relaxed in his arms, I can do that. Tomorrow is another story.

13

I'm back in Summerdale. Caleb's still in the city getting Hugo settled in. He'll be back tomorrow night. The world feels different somehow. *I* feel different—sparkly and full of promise. I've never described myself as sparkly before. Ha! Maybe it's the Christmas lights and decorations all over town, or maybe it's the first man to ever really make me *feel*.

I head over to the quiet study space in the second-floor loft of the Summerdale library to meet my student, Olivia, a fourth-grader struggling in math. She's not here yet. I spot Caleb's older brother Drew browsing the shelves over in the biography section. He turns, a thick book in his hands, and spots me, jerking his chin.

I figure I should get to know Caleb's family better, so I attempt conversation. "What're you reading?"

He walks over to show me the cover. A biography on General MacArthur. "I heard you were back working at your dad's place. How's he doing?"

"Good." *Has Caleb mentioned me?* "You read a lot of military bios?"

He looks a little sheepish. "Finally got a library card, so now every week I read either a bio on a famous general or a military history."

"I'm trying to get him to branch out," Audrey calls out playfully from the stairs on her way up.

He turns. "When you find something more interesting than military strategy, I'll consider it."

Audrey joins us. "Hi, Sloane, please tell Drew there's more to reading than military strategy." She turns to him. "It's called a good story."

"I don't read much, so I don't feel qualified to say," I admit.

Audrey gasps. "Blasphemy. You both should come to book club on Tuesday night, right here in the library. Our selection for the week is on the display right up front. It's a story about a movie star from the silent film era and her career challenges when talkies first became a thing."

"I'm pretty busy with tutoring, work, and Winterfest," I say.

Audrey's not paying any attention to me. Instead she's lifting her chin toward Drew, a challenge in her eyes.

He cracks a smile. "I'm not going to be the only guy at your book club. There's a reason it's all women. The books don't appeal to guys. Talkies?"

She wags a finger at him. "One day I'll get you there, and you'll see, a good story can be just as interesting, no, *more* interesting than a battle."

"Life's a battle," he returns. "There's no greater lesson than what I learn right here." He taps the book. "Now are you going to check me out, or do I have to deal with the excruciatingly slow Martin over there?"

She beams a smile, turns, and heads downstairs. He follows her.

Jenna told me their story. She says Audrey has had a thing for Drew since she was a kid. Seems like they're at least on more even footing now, approaching friend level, which is better than they used to be. Audrey sent many excruciatingly sappy emails to Drew when he was away on military duty. I can relate to the older-guy crush. Thank God I never sent anything to Max when I was in the throes of teen adoration.

He'd never let me live it down. Real classy of Drew to let it slide.

Caleb is much warmer and sweeter than Drew. I smile to myself, thinking of him. I saved a picture of us from the photo shoot. I tap on my phone to view it again. Dmitri captured something I hadn't been conscious of before—an undeniable chemistry between us. We look so happy together.

Oh, man, do I have it bad. Well, can I help it? He absolutely *floored* me, saying he wanted to marry me the first time we went out. No wonder I got in so deep so fast. One week, and I'm already falling. That's never happened to me before. Is it real? Only time will tell.

I sure hope so.

~

A week later—as a result of poor judgment, and Kayla and Audrey ambushing me—I'm dressed as an elf at the pancake breakfast with Santa. I might've wiggled out of being an elf, which they claim I'm perfectly suited for due to my short stature (just like them), except they actually bought me an elf hat with attached pointy ears. I couldn't let it go to waste. Okay, I love being included with them. It's the first time I've had female friends.

So here I am, elfing it up the Saturday before Christmas. *Ho-ho-ho*, or whatever elves say. *Jingle-jingle-jingle?* I'm jingling big time today. I look frigging ridiculous. This morning Kayla showed up bright and early at my house with the rest of my costume—a green velvet dress with candy-cane buttons down the front, white tights, and red velvet shoes that not only curl up on the toes, they also have jingle bells. Every time I move, I jingle. It's impossible to blend in like this, which is something I've tried hard to do ever since I stepped out of the modeling spotlight.

How did I get conned into this mortifying event?

"What's wrong?" Kayla asks me.

We're in the elementary school cafeteria. The three of us are sipping coffee, waiting for everything to get set up before the doors open for the kids. A few volunteers are getting the pancake batter ready.

"Are your elf shoes too tight?" Audrey asks with real concern.

"No," I say, lifting a shoe. "They're roomy."

"You look adorable," Kayla says. "We all do. Let's take a pic." She holds up her phone and snaps a selfie with the three of us.

She turns to me. "You didn't smile."

"It's hard to smile when I look absurd," I say between my teeth.

"Why do you care so much what you look like?" Kayla asks.

"I don't." *Do I?* It suddenly hits me that I've been so sensitive about being judged for my looks that I can't bear for people to look at me. I'm *still* trying to hide like I did back in high school, wearing all black, except now I hide in baggy sweaters and coveralls.

Kayla wiggles her elf ears on the sides of her green hat with her fingers. "We're supposed to be the jolly elves, like the court jesters of the Santa court."

"It's for the kids," Audrey says. "We're part of the Christmas magic."

I nod, trying to get into it and not worry about how I look.

"Come on, let's practice," Kayla says, holding up her phone for another selfie. She takes them in rapid succession, orchestrating the photo session. I respond instinctively, used to direction for pictures. "Silly face! Happy face! Kissy face!"

"Wait, I elfed up that last one," Audrey says.

We crack up. Just like that, I relax.

The rest of the day we keep bringing back that classic "elfed up."

Santa elfed up.

The reindeer tipped over. What an elfed-up situation!

We elfed things up to the next level.

Our infectious laughter and smiles seem to bring out the best in everyone. The parents seem relaxed waiting in line with their kids, Santa (aka Nicholas from the Summerdale Mart) is in his element, and the pancakes are a big hit.

After Santa's shift ends, Kayla, Audrey, and I do a dance for the kids, linking arms and kicking up our legs like the Rockettes to the tune of "Holly Jolly Christmas."

Like a magnet, my gaze is drawn to the front door, where Caleb just stepped in. He's smiling and starts clapping along in time. The parents and kids pick up on it, clapping along.

We finish and take a bow. Kayla throws an arm around us both. "This can be our new tradition. The three shorties of the group bringing elf magic."

"That would be elfing terrific," Audrey quips.

"Or truly elfed up," I say.

We laugh. It's fun to have an inside joke. I so rarely was in on it growing up.

"My stockings ripped during the kick routine," Audrey says, hurrying to the back of the cafeteria, where the restrooms are. She likes to be neat and modestly covered.

"I'll walk around for photo ops," Kayla says. "You want to join me?"

"Uh…" I can't tear my gaze away from Caleb as he makes his way over to me, his eyes intent on mine, a small smile playing around his lips.

"I see you might be busy," Kayla says, giving my arm a squeeze. "Have fun!"

"Thanks, I'll see you later." I belatedly remember how ridiculous I look and shuffle my feet, accidentally bringing more attention to myself with the jingling elf shoes.

"Hello, elf," he says warmly.

My cheeks heat. "I look silly."

"You looked perfectly comfortable dancing with Audrey and Kayla. Nice high kicks, by the way."

I tuck my hair behind my ears and feel the felt pointy elf ears. "I kinda forgot to be self-conscious about the outfit for a while there. The kids were enjoying it so much."

"Hey, you weren't you, you were an elf. Did you tell Santa what you wanted for Christmas?"

I laugh. "No. Kids only for Santa's lap. I guided them to the big guy and gave out holiday coloring books."

He takes both my hands in his. "Tell me your wish later."

It occurs to me he's thinking of Christmas, only a week away. "You don't have to get me a present."

"Same for you." He leans down to my ear. "Besides, you're the best present I could ever have wished for."

I stare at him, speechless. My throat nearly closes with emotion. I never thought a guy would open his heart like this to me. And I definitely never anticipated feeling so much so fast.

He gets serious. "Just in case I'm not the same for you, I'd better get you that present."

"No, you are."

We gaze into each other's eyes for a charged moment. The happy tune of "Rudolph the Red-Nosed Reindeer" fades away; the sound of the crowd, nothing exists in that moment but me and Caleb.

He gives me a peck on the cheek. "Can you keep the costume a little longer?"

I grin. "You have a secret elf fantasy?"

He gives me an appreciative once-over. "I do now."

I shake my head. "I'll go change, weirdo." I head toward the cafeteria restrooms.

"Think about it!" he calls.

I walk with an extra jingle in my step.

Caleb

Things are heating up at the Winterfest committee meeting, and I don't mean because it's only four weeks away. Max is glued to Sloane's side as they work out the details together on the coronation and parade to the ball. Audrey is at the far end of the table from Max, which I'm guessing is on purpose. I know I shouldn't let it bother me that Sloane is so close with Max. They finish each other's sentences and laugh at inside jokes. I console myself that I'm the one Sloane spent most of the last two weeks with. We meet up regularly for dinner, and she even invited me to dinner with her dad at their house. That means she takes us seriously.

I'm on Sloane's other side, waiting for her attention. I agreed to help plan the ball with her. Not that I know much about balls, but I can make phone calls to vendors as well as the next guy. My schedule's flexible, if erratic, between work at the dojo and modeling gigs.

Jenna, Mrs. Peabody, Nicholas, and Audrey are talking about indoor activities to add to the festival, including a Dog's Got Talent contest, which I'm definitely entering Huckleberry in. He'll sweep the prizes. Smartest, most athletic, best coat, Huckleberry's got that locked up.

Finally, Sloane turns to me. "I think we got the logistics worked out. Max volunteered a flatbed truck and his pickup truck for the royal court to ride in the back, all decorated, to get them from the coronation to the ball. Isn't that great?"

Max's shoulders draw back as he puffs out his chest. "Your chariot awaits, my lady."

Sloane pushes his shoulder. "Not *my* chariot. Whoever gets crowned queen."

"It should be you," Max and I say at the same time.

I scowl at him.

He lifts one shoulder in a careless shrug. "We agree. She's a queen."

Sloane looks between us, her brows furrowed. "*Not*. So anyway, Caleb, we need to find a caterer that's reasonably priced."

"The Horseman Inn always contributes food to the festival. I could see if they'd be willing to do it."

Max holds up a finger. "Or…we use the caterer at the Bell estate. Aren't they set up for this?" The Bell estate is our ball venue, frequently rented out for events.

"They're very expensive," Sloane says. "I convinced them to let us use the space without using their caterer because it's a charitable event."

"I'll talk to them," Max says. "I might be able to get them on board with an offer to work some landscape design for them. Their place could use a more modern appeal, especially by the front drive."

"You would?" Sloane exclaims. "That would be great."

I can top that. "If that doesn't work out, I'm sure I could get The Horseman Inn on board. The new chef, Spencer, is brilliant."

"Sure, thanks, Caleb," Sloane says absentmindedly. She goes through a list she has on her phone, doling out tasks to me and Max. Somehow all of his tasks require follow-up with her, which means they'll be talking a lot. She sees him at work too.

"You've got a lot on your plate," I say to Max. "Maybe you should share the load."

"With you?" he asks, an edge to his voice.

Sloane looks to Max and then me with a worried look in her eyes. I'm not going to smack him, just keep him in his place.

"Me, Audrey, whoever," I say in a calm, even tone.

Audrey turns at her name and frowns. "I'm swamped."

"I don't mind helping you out," Max says to her. "We haven't had a major snowstorm in a while, so business is slow."

"That's okay," she says tightly.

"Don't be too proud to ask for help," Mrs. Ellis barks. The General is a retired third-grade teacher known for barking out commands. "Max, that's kind of you. I knew bringing you on board was a good idea. Now the two of you take this over to the study area and work out an equitable distribution of work."

Max stands and gestures toward the door for Audrey to go ahead of him.

Audrey sends Jenna a *rescue me* look.

Jenna smiles. "You could use the help, Aud. I know how busy you are helping me with my wedding planning, Winterfest, leading book club, and running the library."

Audrey mumbles something under her breath, grabs her phone and notepad, and walks out of the room. Max follows.

We can see them through the glass walls of the conference room.

Audrey sits at a long table, and Max sits on top of it, right next to her. She's looking up at him with fire in her eyes, saying something. Probably telling him to take a seat. He turns a chair around and straddles it, facing her.

"I swear if I didn't give these young people a nudge, no one would ever take a chance on love," Mrs. Ellis declares.

Everyone laughs.

"I'm serious," she says. "I had to nudge Harper, then Sydney, then Jenna, and now Audrey. Max is a fine young man, who owns his own business."

"Maybe someone should give you a nudge, Joan," Nicholas says with a warm look in his eyes.

I stifle a laugh. Is Santa making a pass at the General?

Mrs. Ellis smooths her short hair. "Nonsense, my husband passed. That part of my life is over. Now back to business."

I lean close to Sloane. "She didn't have to nudge you. You fell into my arms."

"Ha!" Sloane says. "You pursued me relentlessly."

"I regret nothing."

We share a secret smile that says we're falling. I already fell, and I think she's there too. If only she fit with the modeling part of my life, everything would be perfect. My agent is fielding multiple lucrative offers for me after the Cali Pop campaign. Some of their online ads are out already, and there's buzz over it. I want that life and this hometown life too. I've juggled it so far, but never with a serious relationship.

My gut tightens. Sloane is rooted here and was very clear that she's not comfortable with the industry. I get it. But for me, exploring new opportunities in the industry could be something great. Sooner or later, I'll have to choose—pursue the big dream or my dream girl. I don't see a way to have both.

I'll deal with that when the time comes. For now, I'm here and things with Sloane are great.

The meeting wraps up. Sloane spends a good amount of

time talking to Jenna off in a corner, their heads bent close together, voices low. It almost looks like they're hatching a secret plan. Ha! Probably talking about Jenna's wedding.

At least I hope so. Jenna's not beyond a little scheming. And what do Jenna and Sloane have in common? Me.

14

Sloane

I've never been to a wedding in someone's home before. It's New Year's Eve, and we're at Wyatt and Sydney's large home for the marriage of Jenna and Eli. The family room has been cleared of furniture. I'm sitting in a cushioned chair in rows of chairs on either side of a red carpet runner. Up ahead, an arc of silk flowers stands in front of the fire-place for the bridal party. White twinkle lights hang in gentle arcs from the ceiling, giving a soft glow over the space. It's a little before seven p.m. and already dark outside.

Jenna has her sister, Eve, as her maid of honor. Eli has Caleb as best man. They're the two youngest in the Robinson family and are close. They shared a room growing up and, for a while, shared a house too as adults. Eli and Caleb are in place by the arc of flowers, talking quietly with the officiant, Mayor Levi Appleton. Caleb's been a little distant the past couple of days, but I figure he's distracted by wedding stuff.

We're all just waiting for Jenna and Eve to walk down the aisle. There's four dogs here today, Wyatt and Sydney's two dogs, and Jenna and Eli's two dogs. Mocha, the male pit bull, wears a black bowtie while the three girl dogs—pit bull, pit bull mix, and a shih tzu—wear pink bowties. Sydney has them on leash at the end of the aisle. The dogs are lying down with chew toys to keep them busy.

I turn to Kayla at my side. "This is all really nice. I think Jenna had the right idea keeping it small."

"I was just thinking that," she says. "I'm planning a big wedding for me and Adam in June, but I can see the appeal of this too. It almost feels like an elopement, but with her closest friends."

I gaze at Caleb, looking so handsome in his tux, his cheery disposition showing in his every expression. Will we be standing up there one day? Will this start a new tradition in the Robinson family?

"My sisters are looking at property in Summerdale tomorrow," Kayla confides.

"They want to move here together?"

"They're considering opening a bed and breakfast. Brooke is an architect, and Paige is an overworked New York City real estate broker. They like it here and think it might be a good investment. Shh, don't tell. They're still feeling things out."

"If they go in that direction, I can recommend a great landscape designer. Max Bellamy." I text her his contact info and website.

"Awesome," she says. "I hope it works out. Wyatt's been trying to get all of us to move to Summerdale. He got me, though Adam had a lot to do with that. Wyatt's the one who dangled the property in front of them. It's a cute old farmhouse. He knew Brooke would see its renovation potential, and Paige is ready for a break from the constant hustle of her job. Mom says she won't move, but she'd love to be their first guest. It would be so cool to have my family close by, especially once Adam and I start a family."

"Keep me posted."

She smiles and squeezes my arm.

Just then the music starts, and Eve walks down the aisle at a sedate pace. She resembles Jenna, tall and blond, though her features seem sharper. She's wearing a pale lavender dress with satin and lace and holding a bouquet of white roses.

Everyone turns to see Jenna. She's stunning in a sleeveless white gown with beading that catches the light in the bodice. A veil is perched on her head, but I can still see her beaming smile through the thin material as she walks gracefully down the aisle.

Levi welcomes everyone, and then Sydney goes up to read a poem. Audrey follows next. Both poems are about love. I never heard them before since I'm not a poetry person, but they sounded perfect for the occasion.

I watch as Levi leads them through their vows. Both Eli and Jenna are blinking back tears the whole time. I get choked up and nearly cry, but then Caleb catches my eye, and I get control over myself. He winks at me, like he knows I'm this close to bawling. It's just so beautiful. The love between them, the sheer joy they exude, vowing to be together forever. I bet they have beautiful babies. I want babies too. *Sniff*.

"I now pronounce you husband and wife," Levi says. "You may kiss the bride."

Eli cradles Jenna's face with both hands and gives her a kiss. Everyone applauds, and the dogs drop their chew toys to bark along.

Since we're in a home, Jenna and Eli just walk down the aisle and then stay at the other end of the room, toasting each other with the waiting champagne and accepting congratulations. Caleb, Drew, and Adam put away the chairs quickly, storing them in a shed outdoors and returning to bring the furniture back into the family room. Reception time.

And I get to ring in the New Year with Caleb's big happy family, who're feeling more and more like my own.

Caleb catches up to me and gives me a hug. He speaks close to my ear. "One day, darling."

I don't deny it anymore, just return his hug. The idea no longer scares me, only fills me with hope for the future.

∾

Caleb

On New Year's Day, Sloane dashes home early after

spending the night with me, and then texts me an unusual request. She wants me to meet her at Wyatt's place by eleven a.m. and bring Huckleberry for a New Year's celebration with the dogs. *Weird.* Wyatt didn't say anything about that when we were at his place yesterday for Jenna's wedding.

I pull up to Wyatt and Sydney's house at the top of the hill. It's a cool place from the 1920s with gray siding and a gray lighthouse to the right of it. Landlocked, which is the funny part. The lighthouse is actually a water tower dressed up like a lighthouse. There's a lot of cars here already.

I ring the bell, and my sister, Sydney, answers. Snowball, the white shih tzu, is tucked under her arm, and her pit bull mix, Rexie, stands by her side barking. Huckleberry growls low in his throat.

"Hi! Come in!" she yells over the noise. She backs up and says to her dogs, "Stand down."

They get quiet, wagging their tails and sniffing Huckleberry. They've all met before. This is just the standard someone's-at-the-door protocol.

"What's up?" I ask. "There's a lot of cars here. Sloane said eleven, and I feel like I'm late to the party."

"Right this way," she says over her shoulder, gesturing for me to follow.

I take off my jacket, leaving it on the coat rack by the door, and head in the direction of all the noise. They must be in the family room that runs the length of the back of the house. It's a nice space with lots of floor-to-ceiling windows overlooking a backyard of lawn bordered by woodlands.

I stop short at the entrance to the room, my jaw dropping. The furniture is cleared out, and the place is packed with people and dogs.

"Surprise!" Sloane exclaims.

I rub my jaw. "I can't believe it."

She bounces over and hugs me. "Are you happy? I wanted to do something special for you."

I blink a few times, still in shock. Dmitri the photographer is here, set up with the same backdrop and setup he did for the charity calendar. My brothers—Drew, Adam, and

Eli—are here, each of them with a dog. Drew holds the leash for Eli's dog Mocha. Eli has his other dog Lucy. My brother-in-law Wyatt's here, Max, Mayor Levi, Spencer, the chef from The Horseman Inn, and the vet Dr. Russo. The wives and girlfriends are here too. Guess it was lucky for me that Jenna and Eli don't leave for their honeymoon until tomorrow.

"We're finishing your calendar with locals," Sloane says. "I found eight guys willing to pose with a dog."

Dr. Russo approaches. "I brought some extra dogs from the shelter for Max, Levi, and Spencer to pose with. I can't thank you enough for the fundraising to expand the shelter. We'll get there with the help of people like you."

My eyes water. All this time I thought my brothers, local people too, didn't think much of what I do. I thought they thought I was just a pretty face, no substance, but here they are willing to help me out.

I lift my arms wide. "Thanks for coming, everyone. I appreciate it."

"Your woman let us know how important it is to you," Wyatt says.

I wrap an arm around Sloane. My woman. "She's right. It's all for a good cause. I have to warn you, we already have the first four months covered with, uh, shirtless models posing with their dogs, but—"

The guys whip off their shirts. Well, that was easy. The women break into applause, which gets the dogs excited, and they start running around the room. Everyone except Dr. Russo's Boston terrier, who merely lies there, one ear cocked.

"Grab the leashes," Dr. Russo says. "Don't let them get too wound up."

It's chaos with everyone running in different directions, the leashes flying behind the dogs. Sloane chases Huckleberry, who's jumping among the dogs playfully. Dr. Russo helps, producing a container of biscuits, shaking it, and letting out a sharp whistle. Pretty soon the dogs are sitting in a line, waiting for their treat.

Jenna starts spritzing the shirtless guys with baby oil.

Sydney approaches with makeup, but no one wants it. That's fine. Dmitri will make the photos look good.

I walk over to Dmitri, clapping him on the back. "Thanks for coming all the way out here, man."

He smiles. "We didn't finish the job. Always got to see it through."

"Still, I'll cover your fee."

"Already taken care of."

"Sloane?"

"Who else?"

I look over at Sloane smiling at me, her amber eyes sparkling.

I walk over to her and kiss her.

She beams. "At least this time we have multiple dog wranglers instead of just me."

I lean down to her ear. "I'll pay you back for Dmitri. I know he's not cheap."

She shakes her head. "I can afford it. I've been living at home for months. No expenses."

I can't imagine she makes that much as a mechanic, but I'm not going to push away her gift. I'll do something nice for her later.

Dmitri calls for the first volunteer, and Drew steps up, leading Mocha.

Sloane and I watch, my arm around her shoulders, her arm around my waist. One small niggling worry buzzes around my brain. I'm glad Sloane has everything she ever wanted right here in Summerdale. Problem is, I'm not sure that I do. I've been putting off talking to her about it, but I gave my agent the go-ahead for a major campaign starting at the end of the month. It'll take me far from home with multiple commitments down the line as their brand ambassador. I need to get Sloane on board. I want it all, even knowing it might not be what she wants. There has to be a way to make it work, right? I can't bear thinking about losing her.

Drew poses with Mocha across his shoulders, his arms lifted to flex his biceps, his ripped chest and abs on full display. He keeps fit. He's not much of a smiler, but when all the women go crazy wolf whistling at him, a small smile plays over his lips.

"Yes!" Dmitri exclaims. "Love it."

Not to be outdone, Eli has his dog Lucy do her trick where she leaps into his arms when he calls her. He laughs as she licks his face.

Dmitri goes crazy, snapping away. Everyone's laughing and having a good time.

Adam's more reserved, which is fine because his English bulldog, Tank, is a lazy dog who just wants to lie down, head on his paws. Kayla runs over with a piece of bacon she brought just for this purpose and coaxes Tank to a sitting position. Adam sits next to Tank and puts his arm around him. Dmitri snaps a picture just when the two of them look at each other up close. It's a great shot.

Spencer, the chef with short brown hair and a winning smile, gets into it, flexing his bicep next to the yellow hound assigned to him. The dog jumps up on him and licks his bicep. I hope Dmitri got that one. The other guys are more sedate. Both Levi and Dr. Russo just stand there—shirtless guys holding dogs in their arms. Dmitri has to coax them to flex a muscle. The women egg them on, and they seem to relax a bit, playing more to the camera.

Wyatt goes last, and he seems prepared, flexing and smoldering at the camera. Only problem is Snowball, being a cute little white shih tzu, looks at odds with all the testosterone he's giving off. It's a really funny contrast.

Dmitri cheers him on while the rest of us fight laughter, exchanging amused looks.

Wyatt finally notices. "What?"

"Nothing, babe," Sydney says. "You are *hot*. Keep it up."

His brows draw down. "I know I'm hot. Where's my catcalls and whistles?"

Sydney gestures for the women to join her as she claps and hoots at him.

"That's better," Wyatt says. He holds up Snowball so they're eye to eye. Her mouth is open, and it kind of looks like she's smiling at him. Wyatt smiles back. "Don't her teeth look great?" Dmitri snaps the pic. Dog and owner smiling at each other.

Sydney shares with the rest of us. "Wyatt brushes Snowball's teeth every night."

"Rexie's too," he says. "Dental hygiene is important for dogs too, especially shih tzus because of their underbite."

Sydney smiles widely. "What he said."

I walk around, thanking all the guys for their help.

"Man, that was hard work," Adam says. "It felt like it took forever to get the picture he wanted, and the whole time I had to look like I was enjoying myself."

I laugh and give him a bro hug. "I know it's not your thing. I appreciate it. You were actually only up there about twenty minutes. I've had twelve-hour shoots."

He claps me on the shoulder. "Better you than me. I didn't realize how hard you worked. I honestly thought it was just a quick picture snap and then you went home." He gestures to all the equipment. "Lighting, backdrops, posing."

It feels good to be understood. "Usually there's hair, makeup, and wardrobe too. It's a whole thing. I know it looks natural in the photos, like we all just walked in off the street, but there's a whole team behind it."

Drew ruffles my hair. "How come you didn't do your thing?"

"Dmitri already got my pic when I first set up this gig. We're good to go."

"Then what's Huckleberry doing here?" he asks.

I look around for him and don't see him. "I'm not sure. I'd better check on him."

I wander through the house, reaching the formal living room up front. There's a Christmas tree in the corner. Sloane sits cross-legged on the floor in front of it with Huckleberry. Dmitri crouches in front of them, taking their picture. I guess Sloane wanted a picture with him.

She beams at me. "It's to go with your Christmas picture collection." She means the photos of my family in front of the

Christmas tree. She wants to be part of my family. My chest tightens.

"Sloane, sweetheart, that's so thoughtful."

"Join us!"

I sit next to her and put my arm around her with a big smile, already imagining this picture as the start of our own Christmas tradition. Warmth floods me at the thought. Me, Sloane, and Huckleberry. Hopefully kids down the line too.

Dmitri takes a few more pictures and then offers Sloane his hand, helping her to her feet. I stand too, giving Huckleberry a rub for being such a good sport.

"I never get tired of taking your picture," Dmitri says to Sloane. "Will you be joining Caleb in Fiji?"

Sloane's head whips toward mine. My stomach drops. Shit. I didn't want her to find out this way. I wanted to find the perfect time to tell her and then hope it didn't mean the end of us. Fiji is just the beginning for me.

Dmitri continues, oblivious. "I'll be there. You'd look spectacular in a tropical setting. White sand beaches, turquoise water, your dark hair and creamy skin. Those eyes." He sounds like he's half in love with her. A photographer's love.

"Uh, I haven't told her yet," I say.

"You're going to Fiji?" she asks. "For what?"

Dmitri backs away. "I'll go pack up. Sorry for spilling the beans."

I give his shoulder a squeeze and face Sloane, keeping my tone even. It's not how I wanted this conversation to happen, but it's here now, so I have to deal with it. "If we can just talk this out, we can make it work."

"Talk what out?"

"Look, I was going to tell you. I had five offers for major campaigns, and my agent was pushing me pretty hard to accept the Fiji assignment. I guess I didn't want to mention it because my career's suddenly exploding, and I know you don't feel comfortable with that scene."

Hurt registers in her eyes. "I'm happy for you. I just thought you would've told me. How long have you known?"

"Two weeks. I've been sitting on the offers, and I told my

agent two days ago that I'd take Fiji. It's for a fragrance by the designer Rafael. Commercials, print, internet campaigns. The shoot's not until the end of January." I take a deep breath. "You're welcome to come along."

She stares at the floor. "I just don't understand why you kept it from me." She meets my eyes. "You told Dmitri. Obviously I know you're trying to book gigs."

I blow out a breath. "I guess I didn't think you'd take it well. There's more. Fiji is just the beginning. I'm supposed to represent the brand at fashion week in Paris. There's a possibility I'd become their representative in a three-year contract." I bite back a smile. It's an exciting prospect. A huge deal for a model.

"Holy crap."

"Yeah."

"So you'll be traveling a lot, then."

"Possibly. If things go my way."

She worries her lower lip. "I'm committed to staying in Summerdale. I finally feel like I have a group of women friends. I'm involved in the community. I'm doing what I love at Dad's shop. I don't want to hold you back, Caleb." She exhales sharply. "It seems like we don't want the same thing."

My gut does a slow roll. I still don't have the answers to making us work. I was hoping she would. "I do want what you want. Eventually."

"When?"

"Once I'm no longer marketable. I don't know when."

Her lips press together. "Once you're a plain ordinary joe, which you'll never be."

"You want me to apologize for my looks?" I say defensively. "I take care of myself. And you—you're beautiful."

"Stop."

I reach to cup her face, but she pulls back. "I'm serious."

"And I'm serious when I say I don't need your pretty words. I was hung up on my looks, or lack thereof, for a very long time, and I'm comfortable in my own skin now. Looks are just one part of the package. For you the package sells and that's okay. I wish you well." Her voice cracks.

My gut lurches. "What do you mean you wish me well?"

She's quiet.

I can barely get out the words over the lump in my throat. "Are you breaking up with me?"

She blinks rapidly, her eyes welling. "I think we both know we're going in different directions. You should be able to go off and enjoy yourself."

"What does that mean? You think I'm interested in other models? I'm interested, no, it's more than that…Sloane, I love you."

"I love you too!" she cries. "But don't you see? This is what love is. Letting the other person be their best self. I'm giving you your freedom. I'm sure you'll soar."

"Bullshit. I don't want this."

She wipes tears from her cheeks. "Ask yourself why you didn't tell me your big news for two weeks. It's not because we didn't spend lots of time together. There were so many opportunities for you to say something, but you didn't because you knew our paths were diverging."

I tense, my gut a sickly knot. *Is she right? I couldn't see a solution, and maybe that's because there isn't one.*

She stands there, staring at me for a long moment, her eyes still shiny with tears.

"Sloane."

"Goodbye, Caleb," she says softly.

I watch as she walks out the door, taking my heart with her. No, this can't be happening. After this huge gesture where she brought my two worlds together, she breaks my most important world apart. Us.

I start after her and then stop and shove a hand through my hair. I'm set to launch a globe-trotting career while she's tied to home. Our paths *are* diverging, like she said. I don't want to hurt her with a lot of back and forth. Together, apart, together, apart.

My eyes sting with tears, my chest tight. If only love were as simple as that first thunderbolt.

15

Sloane

It's been two days since Caleb and I had our amicable breakup. All in all, I think we handled it very maturely. If only I didn't feel like complete and utter crap. I arrive at work on Monday morning to find Dad's not here yet. Max has off today. He had to restock on rock salt and sand for snow plowing. They're predicting more snow in our area soon.

Dad's probably picking up donuts for us at Jenna's shop. He regularly does that on a Monday to get us going. I wouldn't mind drowning my sorrows in sugary sweet goodness. I sigh and get to work, hoping to lose myself in it. There's a 1978 Cadillac Coupe de Ville here in need of new brakes. I wonder who this car belongs to. Still has the original sea green mist paint job and is in pretty good condition. I'll look it up later when I get to invoicing.

I get the car in place for the hydraulic lift and send it on up. Just as it finishes, I hear the shop's phone ring.

Guess Dad's not back yet. I wipe my hands on a rag and walk over, but the phone stops ringing. Should I check the voicemail, or let Dad take care of it later? Meh, he can deal with it. I need a distraction.

An hour later, I finish with the new brake pads and rotors and lower the car. Damn, it's so quiet. Dad's still not here?

I walk over to his office, but he's not there either. A prickly feeling crawls along my spine. This isn't like him. He's a dependable hard worker who never misses a day of work. The only time he closes the shop is for holidays and my graduation.

I pull my phone from my pocket and stare at the screen. I had it on silent and missed a call from a number I don't recognize. I listen to the voicemail. "Hi, this is Deborah. I'm a nurse at Eastman Hospital. Your father's been admitted. He gave us this number to contact you."

I immediately grab my purse and the shop's keys, lock up, and race to my car. I peel out of the lot. The hospital is about twenty minutes away. He's been admitted. Why? What happened? I should've called and asked, but it seemed more important to get there. He can't die. He's my rock, the one thing I can count on in this world.

Please, please let him be okay.

I get to the hospital and end up parking far away. The lot is packed. I run at full speed to the entrance and burst into the waiting room.

I rush to the front desk. "I'm Sloane Murray. My father was admitted earlier. I need to see him. Is he okay?"

The nurse, a brunette in her fifties, looks at me. "Slow down. What's your name again?"

"Sloane Murray. Please, my dad." I tap the counter. "Rob Murray. Robert Murray. I need to know if he's okay. I need to see him right away."

She looks his name up on the computer. "He's up in the cardiac unit. Let me check if he can have visitors."

"Why couldn't he?"

Every worst-case scenario runs through my head. Cardiac. They could be zapping him with those paddles like you see on hospital emergency room shows on TV, or prepping him for surgery. My stomach drops at my next thought. My grandfather, dad's dad, died of a heart attack in his forties. Dad's fifty-one. I can't let myself think the worst. Adrenaline races through me. I'm about to burst out of my skin.

She puts the phone down. "Visitor is okay. Let's get your driver's license, and I'll get you a visitor pass."

Five excruciating minutes later, I'm on my way to the elevator. I punch the button. *Come on, come on.* A few other visitors join me in the wait. Finally, the doors open, and we all head inside. I have to wait for the second- and third-floor stops for them. Dad's on the fourth. As soon as the doors open, I rush out, looking for his room.

I find it and walk into a room with an elderly man in it. I walk farther into the room, looking beyond the hospital curtain. Empty. There's not even a bed.

No, no, no. Tears blur my vision. *Where is he? What's wrong?*

A moment later, a bed appears, being pushed into the space. I hurry out of the way. It's Dad. He has an oxygen tube in place in his nose and an IV in his hand.

"Just returning from a test," the nurse says. "He passed with flying colors." The nurse is a cheerful-looking young guy, who reminds me a little of Caleb with his crew cut. I wish Caleb were here with me.

"Sloane," Dad says weakly.

As soon as his bed's set in place and the nurse leaves, I give him a gentle hug. "Dad, what happened?"

He puts a hand on my head. "I'll be okay. The doctor says it was a minor heart attack, and I don't need surgery at this point. She's putting me on blood thinners. That's the good news."

My stomach lurches. "What's the bad news?"

He makes a face. "She wants me to exercise and switch to a heart-healthy diet."

"Dad! Oh my God, you scared the crap out of me. You'll do everything the doctor says. I'll make sure of it. I'll find out what's involved and make it happen."

"Is Max at the shop?"

"I'll text him right now. He was just picking up supplies for the coming storm."

I text Max and let him know the deal. He promises to be at the shop within the hour. I lift my head. "Max is on his way to the shop. All covered, so you can relax."

He closes his eyes. "Good."

"When did this happen? You seemed fine this morning at home."

He keeps his eyes closed. "On my way to get donuts. I had this shooting pain in my chest and pulled over. I thought maybe it was heartburn, but then it kept getting worse, and I broke into a cold sweat, feeling dizzy. I managed to call 911. Next thing you know, I'm racing here in an ambulance. One of the nurses said she'd get a hold of you for me."

I shake my head, tears stinging my eyes. "No more donuts. We're going to get you back in fighting form."

He pats my hand, and then his hand stills. I watch his chest carefully. He's still breathing. Just asleep.

Tears stream down my face, and I turn away, looking out the window. I don't want him to see me upset. I was so afraid I'd lose him just like he lost his dad. This is one of those times it's hard to be an only child, bearing the pain alone. Max is busy. My new friends are at work, I'm sure. I text Caleb and let him know what happened and where I'm at. He's the one I really want, even though we broke up.

My throat tightens as I add, *Can you come to the hospital?* I give Caleb the address and room number.

I stare at my phone, hoping he gets the message. I could call. A text appears.

Caleb: *On my way.*

My hand flies to my mouth, covering a sob. I text a quick thank you and collapse in a nearby chair. I watch Dad sleep peacefully after his tumultuous morning. He's always been a big guy, but as he got older, he put on more weight. It must've been a strain on his heart. Or maybe all the fried food clogged his arteries. Dad loves his French fries and potato chips. I'll talk to the doctor to find out the medical details. In the meantime, I just need him to get better.

Caleb arrives a half hour later. I stand, so grateful he's here after our falling-out. I really thought I was making the right decision for both of us, but now all I want is to hang onto him and never let go.

He wraps his arms around me, stroking my back. "So sorry. Is he going to be okay? Are you okay?"

I lift my head. "Yes to both." I fill him in on the details.

His eyes are intent on mine. "I could help. I'm all about nutrition and exercise."

But we broke up. "I can't ask that of you."

"You don't have to ask. I'm happy to do it. I don't leave for four more weeks. Plenty of time to get him on the right track."

I nod and then burst into tears.

He holds me close. "Shh, it's going to be okay. Everything's going to be all right."

I want to believe him more than anything, so I do.

The nurse comes in to check Dad's vitals, and he wakes up.

I smile at him. "Hi, Dad. Caleb came to visit."

"Hi," Dad says. "Seems I napped through most of your visit."

"No problem," Caleb says.

The nurse finishes and tells Dad he's leaving his shift, but another nurse will be in soon followed by the doctor.

Dad grumbles okay. As soon as the nurse leaves, he says, "They never let you rest at the hospital. Always poking you and checking stuff. He just checked me an hour ago."

I smile because he sounds more like his grumbly self. "Then your job is to get better so we can get you out of here."

"I'd like to help," Caleb says.

"He has a degree in exercise science and knows all about nutrition," I say.

"That's nice of you," Dad says to Caleb. "But not necessary. I'm sure I'll be fine with just a few tweaks to my diet."

"Dad, it would mean a lot to me to have Caleb on board. Of course you should work with the team here, but once you get back home, we'll be your team."

Dad sighs. "Look at you, Sloane. Hometown boyfriend,

local kids for tutoring, pancake breakfast, Winterfest, did I miss anything?"

"I also go to ladies' night, and Audrey's trying to get me to join book club," I say.

"You're putting down roots." He closes his eyes. "What about your career?"

Now is not the time to upset him. "You're tired. Rest."

I sit and hold Dad's hand while he sleeps.

Caleb settles into a cushioned chair across the room.

"You don't have to stay," I say.

"Course I do. He's my rehab client."

Tears sting my eyes. "Thank you."

I made a serious miscalculation cutting ties with Caleb. I just don't know how to make a future with him work.

Dad's been home for four days now, and I feel good about his progress. He's settled into a nice routine at home, sounding more and more like his old self. Caleb set up a health tracker app on Dad's phone. I'm touched by his care. Of course, Caleb lost both parents—his mom to a car accident and his dad to late-stage cancer—so given the chance to set my dad on a better path that will help him live a long life, he's all over that. Dad likes him too. I'm secretly glad for the buffer. I think Dad finds it easier taking orders from Caleb. My job is to see that Dad follows through.

I cleaned out all the tempting food that's not good for him. Out went the chips, cookies, soda, ice cream, and a stack of frozen dinners that looked junky. The key is to be sure he doesn't stop for fast food for dinner. He's big on burgers and fries. I sent both his and Max's beer to Max's place.

I fix us dinner, one of the heart-healthy recipes Caleb gave me—pan-seared steak with herbs and escarole.

Dad stares at his plate. "The steak part I like. What's all this green stuff?"

"Escarole."

"Looks like weeds."

I sit across from him with my own serving of dinner. "It's like kale, only more interesting."

"Caleb's recipe?"

"Yes. How do you think he stays in tip-top shape? You'll be like him soon, fit and healthy. Remember what he said? Within a month, you'll have newfound energy that'll make you feel ten years younger."

He scoffs. "If I were *thirty* years younger, I still wouldn't look like him."

I laugh. "Maybe not. The important thing is you're healthy."

We dig into the steak. It's really good, if I do say so myself.

He finishes his steak and stares at the escarole forlornly. "Thank you for taking good care of me."

"Come on, try it. I promise it's not that bad."

He lifts a dubious brow and takes a bite of escarole. "It does taste better than weeds. There's some kind of dressing on it."

"That's the herbs."

He finishes the greens in a few quick bites like he's trying to get them out of the way. Guess he's not that big a fan.

"It's Saturday night," he says. "You should go out."

"I like hanging with you."

"You're hovering. I'm feeling much better."

"Dad, it's only been five days since your heart attack."

"It was minor. I'm going to watch the Turbo channel and relax. I have your number. I know you'd like to spend time with Caleb." We both love the Turbo channel, which features all cars all the time.

"He'll be here tomorrow night to make Sunday dinner. I can stay and watch TV with you."

"Go, please." He lifts his brows. "I like him."

"Me too."

I take a bite of escarole, debating if this is a good time to tell him I want to stay here in Summerdale working with him, but I'm not sure if the timing is right. Then again, Dad's only going to need me more at work the older he gets. At some point, he'll want to retire, right?

I put my fork down. "Dad, I have a confession."

His head jerks up. "You're pregnant."

"No! Why would that be your first thought?"

"I don't know. Because of the way Caleb looks at you." He wags a finger. "And vice versa."

I clear my throat. "Yes, well, it's not that. So, you know how much I love working at the shop with you. I've been wanting to take a larger role there, help you with the business side as well as repairs. I really feel like I can be an asset."

"Course you can. That's not the point. I'm doing fine. Least I will be once I get past this forced vacation."

I take a deep breath. "I haven't sent out any job applications."

He stills. "None?"

I shake my head. "I'm sorry I misled you about that. I just feel like, college degree or not, working at the garage is what I want to do. I love it more than anything."

He sighs. "Then what was college for?"

"It was good to learn and stretch myself. I don't regret it, and I can still help tutor kids locally just like I've always done, but Murray's is where I see my future."

He lets out a long breath, eying me across the table.

I'm quiet. I've never lied to him before. Even though I feel a huge weight off my shoulders finally admitting the truth, I know he's not happy about the lying or me wanting to stay on with him at work.

He drinks his water, making a face. "Are you sure there's not more orange soda in the back of the pantry?"

"Gone. Caleb says we can add lemon to your water. Would you like that?"

He props an elbow on the table and rests his head in his hand.

"You're tired. I'll get you back to bed."

"I'm thinking," he grumbles.

"Okay."

He lifts his head. "All this time you've been telling me you can't find a job, and I'm thinking it's because it's a tough economy. Instead it's because you haven't even tried."

"But I did try to tell you how much I wanted to work with you."

He sighs. "I'm not happy with the deception, but I can't say this is a big surprise. You told me over and over that you wanted to stay, but I didn't want to hear it. Sloane, I didn't want this for you. I'll never be able to retire. This is a *work until you die* kind of job."

"With me on board, you'll be able to retire. I'll make sure the finances are in order and do everything I can to boost business."

"I got business."

"If we got more business, I could hire more mechanics. It wouldn't be any more work for you."

He straightens and runs a hand through his hair. "To think, if I hadn't brought you to work with me when you were a kid, none of this would've happened."

"I'm so glad you did."

His eyes go soft. "I know you're capable, and if you're sure this is what you want—"

"I'm sure."

He offers his hand. "Then welcome aboard, partner."

I throw my fists in the air. "Thank you, thank you, thank you!" I run around the table to hug him and kiss his cheek. "You won't regret it."

He smiles. "My girl. Best mechanic in the world."

"I learned from the best."

"Love you."

"Love you too, Dad." I return to my seat. "Mom would be rolling her eyes about now. She always thought I was odd for working in the shop."

"Not her thing."

"I know. She's more about the beauty pageant circuit, the modeling. I sure disappointed her there. No career, no Mom."

"Sloane, you don't think that's why she left, do you?"

My lips part in surprise. "Well, yeah, it was that, and I guess you two had troubles."

"She met someone she thought was the love of her life. It had nothing to do with you."

My heart races, and I can't seem to get a breath. A dizzy feeling comes over me, the room blurring before my eyes. Modeling ended. Mom left. I connected the dots all wrong.

"Sloane, you're pale. Take a breath."

All this time I thought I disappointed her in the worst way. She said I was the only reason she stayed as long as she had.

It wasn't my failure that caused her to leave. Could this possibly be true?

Dad reaches across the table and grabs my hand. "Sloane," he says sharply.

I blink a few times, refocusing on him. "But she left a month after my modeling career ended."

He nods, still holding my hand, his eyes gentle. "Granted, she was disappointed. She had high hopes for you, but then she threw herself into self-improvement when your career ended. She always needed a focus. So she met a guy at some kind of spiritual retreat, and they believed they were soul mates. She moved to London with him. They broke up three months later, but she stayed because she liked it there."

My voice comes out shaky. "I never met any guy from London."

"Because they ended so quickly."

I stare at him, my brain slowly absorbing the truth—it wasn't my awkward odd-duck stage that drove Mom away, disappointing her. She followed some guy across the ocean. If she truly believed they were soul mates, I can almost understand. I would never leave a daughter of my own, but I have an inkling of that kind of powerful love.

All this time. All my secret shame.

I break down in tears, dropping my head in my hands, the sobs coming from deep inside. I thought I had no tears left over her, but they won't stop coming. And then Dad's beside me, pulling me close to sob into his chest.

"I'm so sorry, Sloane. If I'd known you believed it was your fault, I would've explained. I should've talked to you about it. I thought talking about her leaving would just upset you."

I'm crying too much to reply.

"So sorry," he croons. "Never your fault. You're perfect just the way you are."

When my tears finally subside, I straighten and wipe my cheeks. "I'm not perfect."

He pinches my chin. "To me, you are. The best daughter a dad could ask for."

"You're the best dad. You've always been there for me. You made me partner."

"That was all you, pushing your way in at the shop." He smiles. "But I'm glad you did."

I take a deep calming breath, finally free from the burden that ruled my life. Mom leaving wasn't my fault. And now I'm finally living the life I was meant to have. Partner at Murray's.

Hopefully, Caleb will want to stay part of my life too.

16

"I'm partner in Murray's!" I exclaim the moment I walk in the door of Caleb's apartment later that night. I feel so much lighter now.

Huckleberry barks excitedly, jumping up on me. I pat him and share the joy with him too. "I know, exciting, right?"

Caleb orders him to sit and then grabs me in a hug that lifts me off my feet. "Congratulations!"

I beam, happiness bubbling up inside me. "Thanks. Dad and I had a good talk. He finally listened and understood this is what I want to do with my life."

"That's awesome." He takes my hand and leads me to the sofa. Once we're settled there, he asks, "How's your dad?"

My heart squeezes. This is the first time we've been alone since our breakup, and he just welcomed me back with open arms, sharing in my big news. After everything he's done for my dad and the way Caleb's been there for me, I know I made a huge mistake cutting things off.

I smile, gazing into his warm hazel eyes. "Good. He's getting better every day. I so appreciate everything you're doing for him."

He takes my hand and gives it a squeeze. "I'm happy to help."

"I don't want to break up," I blurt. "It was a huge miscalculation on my part. Can we pick up where we left off?"

He lifts my hand and kisses the palm. "We already are."

"Just like that?"

"Just like that. And to prove it, I found a really gory horror movie for us to watch. I'm open to your favorite things."

He grabs the remote and clicks over to the movie. His openness makes me think I need to be more open to his way of life too. Another talk we need to have, but not now. It's been an exhausting week between the aftermath of the breakup and Dad's heart attack.

I lean my head against his shoulder, and he wraps his arm around my shoulders, tucking me against his warm side. I relax for the first time in days.

Next thing I know the movie's over and my head's in his lap. I open my eyes, blinking up at him.

He smiles and smooths my hair back. "You fell asleep at the goriest part."

I sit up. "Guess I haven't been sleeping that well at home, listening to every sound in case Dad needs me. Plus I had a big cry earlier when Dad explained Mom left because she was in love with some guy I never met. It had nothing to do with me."

He hugs me and speaks in a low voice by my ear. "I always knew it wasn't your fault, but I'm glad you know it too." He leans back, cups my face, and kisses me. "I have a surprise for you. A late Christmas present."

"You do?" He already gave me an oversized cashmere sweater that feels like I'm wrapped in a pillow.

"Yeah, it was delayed. Be right back."

He heads to his bedroom. He really didn't have to get me two things. I only gave him a scarf. I didn't know what level of gift giving we were at in our relationship. I should've known he'd go all out. Mental note: better gift next year. Of course, that's assuming we're together next year. We need to talk about the fact that his career is taking off while I'm rooted here more than ever. I'm partner in Murray's now, and

I'm determined to make it thrive so Dad can one day retire. He's been working there since he was seventeen.

Caleb returns, holding a small gold box with a red bow on top.

I stand, my heart racing. Is this the big proposal? We've been seeing each other for six weeks now and, though it's fast, I feel closer to him than anyone I've ever been with. I love him.

He places the box in my hand. "Open it."

I pull the lid off the box with a shaky hand. Oh. It's not a ring. I'm surprisingly disappointed, and I can't help but wonder if Caleb's taken a realistic look at the future and realized we're not a fit for the long haul.

"Do you like it?" he asks.

I smile and nod. It's a silver necklace with a steering wheel pendant and a small charm with an *S* for my name. A beautiful and appropriate gift.

He takes the necklace and goes behind me, lifting my hair and kissing the nape of my neck. I shiver. He puts the necklace on me and drops my hair.

I turn and face him. "Thanks. It's so nice."

His brows furrow. "You sound disappointed. I thought you'd like it. Especially now that you're partner."

I hug him. "I do. Thank you."

He pulls back, tipping my chin up. "What's wrong?"

"Do you still think about us getting married like you used to?"

"No."

I turn away. "Oh."

He cups my jaw and turns me back to face him. "I don't need to. The moment we slept together, I knew you were on board. I stopped thinking about it entirely. As far as I'm concerned, it was a done deal a month ago."

I give him a watery smile. "Wish someone would've told me."

"It was understood." He sounds matter-of-fact.

"But what about Fiji? What about after that?"

"We'll figure something out."

"But—"

He kisses me, cutting me off. Heat rushes through me, desire pooling low in my belly. It's been forever since we were together. More than a week. I throw my arms around his neck, returning the kiss passionately, my mind shutting down from its endless worry.

He lifts me, never breaking the kiss, and I wrap my legs around him as he carries me to the bedroom. Nothing else matters but this.

The moment we get into the room, he sets me down and shuts the door. Huckleberry's still napping in the living room. Good. Otherwise, he'd be howling to be let in.

Caleb grins. "I took Huckleberry on a run before you came over to wear him out."

I yank his shirt up and off. "Brilliant man."

"Strip," he orders.

"You too."

We strip in record time and slam together again. His hands are all over me, his mouth hungry. He backs me up until the backs of my knees hit the edge of the mattress. I fall backward, and he covers me, his lips demanding on mine, his tongue sweeping inside as his fingers stroke down my throat.

I tear my mouth away. "Condom. Now."

He gives me one last lingering kiss and lifts off me, walking over to the nightstand. "Touch yourself."

I scoot back on the bed, spread my legs, and stroke my fingers lightly and then with more pressure, relaxing into the pleasure. He's on me suddenly, fitting himself between my legs and taking me with one hard thrust. I gasp, my body stretching to accommodate him.

He groans by my ear. "That was so hot I couldn't wait. You good?"

"Yes."

"Good."

He lifts my leg, pushing it up, opening me farther as he thrusts deep. I suck in air. I've never felt anything like this, so open, so completely possessed. He shifts and thrusts again, hitting a spot on the inside that makes me crazed.

I grab his shoulders, my nails digging in. "Caleb. Oh my God."

He does it again, and I cry out, shocked by the intensity. "Yeah, it's good for me too," he says hoarsely. "You're going to come so hard."

My eyes close, my breath coming in short pants as sensation overwhelms me. The pressure builds unbearably, a deep ache. Intense. He pumps harder, faster, pushing me open with each thrust. White-hot sensations pulse through me in endless waves. My fingers lose their grip on his shoulders as I break with a harsh cry, shuddering under him as an explosion of pleasure steals my breath. He rocks into me, taking what he needs, until he goes off with a harsh groan.

He carefully sets my leg back on the bed. Our eyes meet, both of us breathing hard.

"Caleb." I open my arms to him.

He joins me, holding me tight. I cling to him, yearning for even more closeness and never, ever wanting to let go. The real world with all its complications can't touch us here.

One week later, I'm at WinterFest by Lake Summerdale, making sure everything's going smoothly behind the scenes. I'm keenly aware that time is running out before Caleb leaves for his big trip to Fiji and what I anticipate as the start of his new life. Today's a nice break from the increasing dread over saying goodbye because I'm so crazy busy I barely have time to think. All I do is rush from place to place, refilling supplies for games, food, drink, napkins, you name it. Our mailman, Bill, even set up a tamale stand, a special treat, since he usually only delivers tamales with the mail in the spring and fall when he can keep them warm. Just one of the quirky people living in town. Guess I fit in better than I thought. Wyatt's a huge fan of the tamales and set Bill up with a kiosk and warming oven hooked to the generator running the food section.

There was a small parade with the old-timers' band, a few

representatives from the fire department, and a plush snowman mascot waving to the kids around the lake to start us off. The chocolate festival is popular. Jenna set up a white tent with several tables to accommodate people lingering with hot cocoa and any number of chocolate treats—brownies, cookies, fudge, even chocolate cheesecake. The lake is frozen deep enough for ice skating. A few families are skating on it. There's also games for the kids, but mostly they're running around throwing snowballs at each other.

It's not until afternoon that I get a chance to get off my feet. I'm pleased that the charity calendars we put out with the guys and dogs have sold out. We raised five thousand dollars for the shelter. A win! I head over to the big red barn, where they're hosting a Dog's Got Talent contest, another fundraiser for the new animal shelter. I wanted to watch the show, so I'm off duty for the next hour. I spot Max there, setting up a judges' table with help from Levi.

I wave to them, taking a seat on a metal folding chair. There's a few rows of chairs in the back, but mostly the space is open for owners to show off their dogs. A few people are here with their dogs. It doesn't start for another twenty minutes.

Levi goes for a pile of papers with numbers on them and sets them on the judges' table.

"Need any help?" I call.

"All good," Levi says.

Max walks over to me. "Did your dad come out?"

"No, the doctor said two weeks of rest."

"You're strict. He's only two days away from two weeks."

"And that's not two weeks."

He puts a hand on top of my head, an affectionate gesture. "I'm glad he's going to be okay." He looks past me. "Who is that?"

I turn. A woman with long dark brown hair is here with a golden retriever. She's in her twenties, looking serious. I bet she's competitive. I wonder what her dog's talent is. "Don't know her," I say.

Kayla appears and gives the woman a hug, exclaiming cheerfully and then petting the dog.

"Maybe Kayla's sister," I say. "She did mention her two sisters were checking out a property in town."

His eyes never leave her. "Yeah? They want to move here?"

"She said they were talking about opening a bed and breakfast. Come on, we'll go say hi."

We walk over to them. "Hey, Kayla," I say.

"Hi!" She hugs me. "Sloane, Max, meet my sister Brooke, and this is Scout."

Scout immediately rushes to Max, sniffing his jeans. Max gives him a rub on the side, and Scout's tail thumps hard.

"Hi, nice to meet you," I say, smiling at Brooke.

She gives me a small wave, a diamond ring sparkling on her finger. It looks like an engagement ring. "You too. Kayla told me all about your adventure in elving."

I laugh. "It was elfed up."

Kayla elbows me, grinning.

Scout climbs on Max's leg, arching his head up for more pets.

"Scout!" Brooke exclaims, pulling him down. "Sorry about that. He's not usually so aggressive. He must really like you."

Max keeps petting Scout. "I probably smell like chocolate. I just had a brownie. Always makes the women come running." He winks.

She rubs the side of her neck, her lashes fluttering down. "Scout is a boy dog. Besides, chocolate is bad for dogs."

Max shrugs. "I don't know why he's all over me, then."

A black lab arrives, barking excitedly, which gets Scout's attention, who takes off in that direction, pulling Brooke with him.

"Looks like the festivities are starting," I say. "Let's get a seat."

"I'm supposed to organize the contestants," Max says.

"Me too," Kayla says.

"Okay, I'll catch up with you afterward," I say.

I take a seat and watch as more dogs and their owners

come in. Scout keeps pulling to go see Max, taking Brooke with him. Max pets him each time as Brooke looks like she's apologizing. Max seems to be happy about it.

Kayla's by the entrance, taking the entry fee and giving each owner a sign with a number to pin to their shirt. I wave at Caleb here with Huckleberry. He does a little nod, pointing to Huckleberry, like he's sure they're going to win.

I smile and wiggle my hand side to side in a *maybe* gesture.

He tosses his head like he's offended. I laugh.

Just before they're ready to start, Max appears by my side. "This should be interesting."

"Looks like you have a fan. Scout really likes you."

"No idea why. Too bad his owner's engaged because that would've been an easy in. Hey, your dog loves me; we should go out."

"I saw that ring too. Hard to miss."

"Yup." His eyes follow Brooke as she tries to get Scout to sit. Scout's too excited by all the other dogs and keeps sitting and then popping up again to sniff another dog. "Real pretty."

I don't think he means the dog. Too bad Brooke's engaged. Now that I'm deep in love, I want it for my friends too. It's a glorious floaty feeling. As long as you don't think too far ahead in the future. I'm not nearly as confident as Caleb about how we fit long term.

Levi turns on a microphone. "Welcome to Summerdale's first Dog's Got Talent contest. Now I know each and every one of your dogs is special, so everyone will be leaving here today with a special treat, courtesy of our local vet, Dr. Russo. Dog Mom and Dog Dad caps." Kayla rushes up to hand him a black cap. He holds it up. The front reads Dog Mom. Everyone applauds. "All proceeds from today's event will go toward building a shelter at Dr. Russo's place. We want to help as many dogs and cats as possible find a home. Judges, are you ready?"

The judging table is Mrs. Peabody and Audrey, neither

one of them have a dog, so they're impartial judges. They both give a thumbs-up.

Levi lowers his voice in the microphone. "Let's begin in number order. Proceed to the center of the room, do your trick, and then walk to the back. Let's have fun with this. Go, number one."

Jenna goes first, leading Mocha out, who keeps very tightly to her side. First she tosses up a tennis ball, and he catches it. Then another ball. That one falls, but he grabs it from the ground and manages to get both in his mouth. Next she rests a plush puppy on his head and leads him out, smiling at the judges.

A moment later, they hold up their numbers for the scores. A ten from Audrey and a five from Mrs. Peabody. Boy, someone's a harsh judge. That was a good trick.

Huckleberry does his *grabbing of the toys by name* trick, successfully picking out his monkey, ball, and Frisbee. He takes off with the Frisbee so fast Caleb loses his grip on his leash. That sets off a lot of excitement as Huckleberry decides he'd like to show off his Frisbee to the other dogs, who all lunge to get a hold of the coveted toy. Luckily, the rest of the owners keep their dogs at bay, holding onto the leashes.

Caleb finally gets control and leads him out.

I'm afraid his scores aren't so good. There must've been a penalty for losing control. He got a big fat zero from Mrs. Peabody and a five from Audrey, which is probably her version of a zero.

A miniature poodle does a little dance on its hind legs. Two tens for that.

Wyatt's dog Snowball also does a dance on her hind legs, so after that, he coaxes her to roll over to add to her repertoire. She makes it to her back and then jumps up again. Seven and eight.

Adam pulls his English bulldog, Tank, in a red wagon while Tank rests his head on the bench seat in front of him. The ultimate lazy dog. One and nine. I think Audrey gave him points for cuteness.

Eli orders his pit bull Lucy to stay and then walks a

distance away and says, "Come!" She runs full speed and leaps into his arms. Two and ten.

The dogs seem to be enjoying themselves because every one of them shows off to the best of their abilities with jumping catches for Frisbees, a few more rolling overs, and a particularly interesting Chihuahua, who appears to be counting by tapping her front paw. *Genius*.

A few minutes of conferring between the judges and the blue ribbon is announced for the dancing poodle. The crowd claps and cheers for the dogs, who look happy with the attention. A few minutes later, everyone filters toward the exit, getting a cap on the way out. Some even contribute extra money to support the shelter in a box left by the exit.

I catch up with Audrey. "That was awesome."

She smiles. "I had to score high to balance out Mrs. Peabody." She lowers her voice, though Mrs. Peabody left immediately after. "Doesn't she realize people take the scores personally? This is their beloved dog. You can't give them a zero or one."

"I'll judge with you next year."

She squeezes my arm. "Sounds good. So now we've got an hour before the coronation followed by the ball. You do know you've been nominated for Queen Snowflake, right?"

My jaw drops. "What? Who would nominate me?"

"Who do you think?"

Caleb. I can't believe he's embarrassing me like this! He didn't say a word!

I whirl, searching for him. Our eyes meet across the room, and I cross to him.

"Hey, that went well," he says. "Huckleberry would've won if he hadn't gotten carried away with his Frisbee."

"What were you thinking nominating me for queen?"

"You're my queen," he replies calmly.

I grind my teeth. "No one's going to vote for me. I'm not a beauty queen."

"You could be."

"Stop." I cross my arms, hugging myself. "This is so humiliating. I don't want to stand up there with a bunch of beautiful women. People are going to wonder what the mechanic from Murray's is doing there."

He pinches my chin, his eyes intent on mine. "You belong there. Besides, it's not a beauty contest. It's based on community involvement and your willingness to represent the town in parades, fundraisers, all festivals, and school events. All that good stuff. You're perfect for the job."

I pull away. "Why didn't you tell me?"

"I thought it would be a fun surprise."

I narrow my eyes and whisper fiercely, "Don't you remember how upset I was that you didn't tell me about Fiji for two weeks? Please don't keep stuff from me."

"Okay, I swear this is the last time. I thought you would refuse the nomination, and then you'd miss out on this great opportunity. You're always giving back to the community. You should be recognized for it. Look at it as a compliment."

"Hmph." I suppose I didn't share with Caleb the terror I felt going through kiddy beauty pageants. Mom pushed me into that. I don't like being on stage in front of a crowd. "Did you nominate yourself to be king?"

"You can't nominate yourself. Kayla did it for me. She also nominated Audrey, Max, Dr. Russo, and Levi. She got a little excited. Adam refused to do it." That's her fiancé. Can't blame him.

I exhale sharply. "But if you win, that means you have to make appearances over the next year. You don't know if you'll be able to commit to that with your work schedule."

"I'll figure something out if it comes to that."

I pace back and forth, trying to think of a way to get out of it. I stop. "How many people were nominated?"

"Kayla says there were ten nominations for king and twenty for queen."

I calm down a little. That's a lot of candidates. Chances are small that either of us would win. I can just blend in with the crowd. "It's a popularity contest."

"The community votes, but the final judges are the General and Santa." His lips quirk.

He means Mrs. Ellis and Nicholas. Funny how our version

of Santa always insisted us kids call him Nicholas and not Mr. Polski. Maybe to further the Santa connection. Then I remember Mrs. Ellis is keen on helping people find love. "What if Mrs. Ellis tries to get Audrey and Max together? Audrey could get mad and walk away in the middle of her own event!"

He rubs his hands together. "Can't wait to find out."

17

I made a beeline to Kayla after that startling revelation because I can't stand next to a bunch of queen candidates in beautiful clothes wearing my usual baggy sweater and jeans. Even my pencil skirt doesn't seem enough. Kayla came through. So here I am, back in the barn an hour later, wearing her sleeveless red dress. It's a little loose on top because she has bigger boobs, but we compensated with one of her pushup bras. The result is a dip in the fabric that actually shows cleavage. She did my makeup too. At least I'll blend. That's the important part. I stuck to my own black ballet flats, not daring to wear her heels, even though we're the same shoe size.

The barn actually looks nice. It's usually used as a theater for our Standing O theater company, made up of locals. Long benches were brought back in that they normally use for the audience. Purple streamers and twinkle lights hang in arches throughout the space. In the back, there's a curtain suspended from rigging on the ceiling as well as a few spotlights. Behind the curtain is a row of seats for the nominees.

So here I am, behind the curtain, trying not to freak out. I'm so nervous sweat's running down my newfound cleavage and my spine. I'm going to owe Kayla a new dress after I sweat through this one.

There's too many of us, so half of us are standing, the other half sitting. I grabbed a chair because I was a little worried I'd be unsteady on my feet. It's not that I think I'll win. It's that I'm having flashbacks to all the pageants I was in as a kid. The spotlight, the pressure, the high-pitched giggles. Mom urging me on from backstage.

Mom would've been livid that I hadn't been given time to prepare. We were constantly drilling speeches, walking, skipping, even smiling. I'm almost glad I didn't know ahead of time. It only would've given me crazy levels of anxiety.

I'm not going to be chosen. All I have to do is wait my turn, say my name and what I would do as ambassador to Summerdale, and then take my place in line again. Simple.

Caleb's large hand squeezes my bare shoulder. He leans down to my ear. "Love your dress."

"It's Kayla's."

He kisses my cheek. "I know. Relax, your shoulder feels like granite."

"Relaxing on stage is not an option."

"It'll all be over soon."

Except it isn't. First, there's a presentation of the four honors students from the high school—two boys, two girls—who'll be in the royal court. The girls are wearing cocktail dresses, the boys are in suits. They look happy to be there. That would *not* have been me in high school.

Then, it takes forever to get through all the candidates, some of whom have prepared *speeches* for how they'll represent the town. I didn't even know about this until an hour ago. I can't think of anything to say. My mind goes absolutely blank.

Next thing I know, Caleb's nudging my shoulder. "Your turn," he whispers.

I walk up to the mike on unsteady legs. It's too tall for me. I try to pull the mike off the stand, but it seems to be stuck. I pull the whole thing down to my level, mike plus stand. "Hi." Feedback rings out, and the crowd groans. I hold the mike farther away. "I'm Sloane Murray, partner in Murray's. If you don't know the place, we're your local auto repair shop. We also do light bodywork."

It's so quiet I can hear my heartbeat pounding in my ears. I suck in air. "Hope that didn't sound like a plug. I don't know what to say."

I look out into the audience, a sea of faces, all eyes on me. I can't look at the judges. The weight of everyone's judgment is a palpable thing. Mom's voice rings in my head. "Head high, big smile!"

No, that's not me. Not anymore. I'm not about putting on a big fake smile, being judged for my looks. I take a deep calming breath. Here, now, I'm finally in a good place in my life. I'm doing the work I want to do with Dad, deeply in love for the first time, surrounded by friends. And I could only have had this kind of happiness here in Summerdale.

I clear my throat. "This nomination was a surprise. I, uh, grew up here, and I plan to live here for the rest of my life. This community has given me everything I've ever wanted, and I'll give back in any way needed, whether or not you vote for me as queen. I love Summerdale. It's home."

I let go of the mike, and the whole thing topples over, making a huge racket. But it's hardly noticeable because everyone's clapping and cheering. I right it and straighten, my chin high, shoulders back with pride. I did it! I smile and catch the eye of Mrs. Ellis at the judges' table on the side, who's smiling back at me. I let out a satisfied breath and return to my seat.

Caleb gives my shoulder a squeeze, and I put my hand on top of his. I'm not mad about the nomination anymore. He only wanted me to be recognized as a contributing member of the community. I've done my share of free or discounted car repairs, I've been tutoring students in math for free since high school, and I always donate to local causes. Not huge donations, but every little bit counts. And the more I give back to the community, the more it gives back to me. Joining the Winterfest committee and helping with the fundraising calendar was fun and brought me closer to my new female friends. I guess I should just call them friends, right?

Several more candidates go up to talk, and I space out, worn out after all the excitement.

Finally, the last candidate finishes. A few moments later, Mrs. Ellis makes her slow way to the microphone with Nicholas by her side, his hand hovering near her elbow.

She pulls the mike off the stand with a quick jerk. "Thank you to all the candidates for being willing to represent Summerdale as ambassador. Nicholas and I had too many good choices."

Nicholas leans in. "But we thought it best if the king and queen got along since they'll have so many events to go to together."

My gaze shoots to the end of the row, where Audrey's sitting. Mrs. Ellis believes Audrey needs help in the love department, and she and Max seem to be on better terms now. Or maybe she'll try to match Levi with someone, but who? I remember she commented on Levi's lonely bachelor existence. I crane my neck to find him behind me. He looks relaxed, a pleasant expression on his face. It would make perfect sense for the mayor to be Summerdale's ambassador. Maybe that pretty woman next to him. She looks to be in her thirties, but is that a wedding band on her finger?

"Sloane Murray!" Mrs. Ellis announces.

My head whips around. *Me?*

She gestures for me to step forward.

This cannot be happening.

"Everyone give a hand to our first Queen Snowflake," Mrs. Ellis says.

I rise from my seat as applause breaks out. Queen Snowflake. It's so absurd I almost laugh, but I'm too shocked to even crack a smile. I make it to her side, and she nods at me before announcing, "And Caleb Robinson is our first King Frost."

More applause as Caleb bounds forward, dropping an arm over my shoulders. I lean heavily against him.

"Breathe," he whispers in my ear.

"We'll now have the coronation ceremony," Nicholas says. "You might want to get your cameras ready."

I stare out into the audience, expecting looks of surprise or whispers, but all I see are smiles and people holding up their phones to take pictures. No one's questioning me being chosen. Actually, Caleb said the community voted, and then Mrs. Ellis and Nicholas had to agree. They chose me.

I stand taller. All this time I've felt on the outside, the odd duck, yet here I am, a queen. I beam a smile, so happy I almost want to laugh for the sheer joy of it all.

Kayla walks over, smiling. She puts a sash on me and a crown with rhinestones. "You look stunning," she whispers.

"Thanks," I say, still floating in a happy cloud.

She puts a sash and crown on Caleb too before saying, "Stay here. Picture time. The photographer from the *Summerdale Sheet* is here." That's our online newspaper.

As soon as she steps out of the way, the audience breaks into wild applause and whistles. Caleb takes my hand and gives it a squeeze.

And then I smile for many pictures, and for the first time in a long time, being in the spotlight feels good. My shoulders draw back with pride. I love this community, and I feel that love right back. It's a beautiful thing. Today I'm a queen with the king I love, and I'll do everything in my power to help my kingdom.

～

Caleb

I help my queen up to a flatbed truck decorated on the sides to look like a royal carriage. There's two thrones, held in place by brackets in back, borrowed from the Standing O theater company. It's a nice setup. We're taking a slow tour around Lakeshore Drive so everyone can see us before heading over to the venue for dinner and the royal ball. One of Max's crew guys is driving us. Max is behind us, driving his pickup truck with the high school kids in back—two princesses and two princes from the royal court.

I take my seat on the throne and grin at Sloane. "High class."

She smiles. "Sure is. I'm just glad to be outside. Gives me a chance to finally cool off. If you had told me that I'd be the first Queen Snowflake of Summerdale when I was in my goth teen phase, I would've laughed my ass off. Yet here I am, actually enjoying myself." She touches her crown. "I used to look cute in a tiara, but I think the crown's even better."

"You look best naked."

"Shh."

"Hey, maybe later tonight you can wear just the crown. Huh?"

She grabs me by the shirt and pulls me in for a kiss. "You're so cute."

"Ready back there?" the driver says.

"Sure, Dave," Sloane says. "Just take it slow. No seatbelts back here."

"You got it. I'll stick to back roads. It's only a two-mile drive."

He starts up the truck, and it makes a loud cranking noise.

Sloane's brows furrow. "That doesn't sound good."

The truck eases onto the road and makes its slow way to Lakeshore Drive one block over. A crowd has gathered in The Horseman Inn's parking lot, and we wave at them as we pass. More people appear on the decks of the lakeside homes to wave at us.

"My arm's getting tired from waving," Sloane says.

"That's why they invented the royal wave." I demonstrate with just a small movement of my hand.

She laughs and copies me.

For a little while, it almost seems like we are royal. Everyone we pass is smiling and cheering for us. Someone even shouts, "All hail the queen and king of Summerdale!"

The truck makes a slow turn off Lakeshore Drive. Guess our tour is over. Time for the ball. This is going to be awesome.

I jerk as the truck lurches and then stalls. "Uh-oh."

Sloane immediately lifts her dress and climbs out of the truck, jumping down to the ground. She walks around to the driver, talks to him for a minute, and then he pops the hood.

Is my queen going to fix a truck in her fancy dress?

Max gets out of the pickup truck. "What's going on?"

The high school kids stand and peer over at us.

"I don't know," I say. "It just stalled."

He walks over to Sloane, and I follow.

She looks up. "Max, bring me your toolbox. I'll get this fixed in no time."

"I can do it," he says. "You're wearing a nice dress."

She rolls her eyes. "My fingers are small and nimble. This is a tricky spot." She then goes into detail on the repair, which sounds like a foreign language to me, but Max understands and goes to retrieve the toolbox.

One of the high school princesses walks over, filming Sloane with her phone. "You are a badass, Queen Snowflake. You think you could teach me how to fix car stuff?"

Sloane smiles. "Sure, I think everyone should know the basics. If you're really interested, you're welcome to shadow me at work one day."

"Awesome."

Max returns with his toolbox, and Sloane gets to work. It takes her five minutes. I don't even know how she pinpointed the problem so quickly. She took one look and knew what to do.

My woman is brilliant.

She wipes her hands together and shouts, "Start it!"

Dave starts the truck, and it rumbles to life.

Sloane shuts the hood with a satisfied thunk, adjusts her crown, and climbs back into the truck, taking her place on her throne.

The teen girl with the camera follows close behind, so I hang back to stay out of the video. She stops filming and raises a fist. "Woman power!"

Sloane laughs. "It's not hard once you know how. Catch up with me at the ball and we'll talk about a lesson in basic auto repair."

The girl blows her a kiss and goes back to her ride.

I climb into the truck and join Sloane. "You amaze me."

She cocks her head. "Why is everyone so amazed? This is

what I do for a living. I've been working on cars since I was twelve years old."

I kiss her. "I love you."

Her eyes go soft. "I love you too. It's not so bad being queen."

"Get used to it."

The truck begins its slow journey. And I know in my heart of hearts that I never want my journey with this incredible woman to end.

18

Sloane

I'm having an out-of-body experience. I know it's all pretend. Obviously I'm not a real queen, but the way everyone's treating me, it feels very real. We're at the reception hall decorated in gold and purple. When we first arrived, we were presented as the new king and queen as we walked in to massive applause. Someone even used a trumpet sound effect that sounded like a royal announcement.

I knew how the place would be decorated since I helped plan everything. I just never expected to be the one experiencing it. The reception hall has a dance floor in the center surrounded by round tables covered in white tablecloths. At the far end of the room is a raised dais with two large leather cushioned chairs for the king and queen with regular cushioned chairs on either side of them for the rest of the royal court. We were served drinks first, dinner first, and now people keep coming over to congratulate us.

In a break from our royal subjects, I say to Caleb under my breath, "Is everyone in town going to call me Queen Snowflake for the rest of the year?"

"I hope so," he says with a grin.

"What about in the summer?"

"Maybe they'll shorten it to Queen S. Works with your name."

"This is going to take some getting used to."

Audrey announces into a microphone that it's time for everyone to get dinner at the buffet. We royals already ate.

Caleb leans close, speaking near my ear. "Sloane, there's nothing more I want in life than to be with you."

My throat tightens. "I want that too."

"If you'll stick with me, I'll quit modeling after a year and find something that keeps me close to home."

"Oh, Caleb, I don't want you to give up on your dreams because of me."

"*You* are the dream."

My eyes water. "What would you do?"

"I've been giving that a lot of thought. I really liked helping your dad with his rehab. I found out there's some master's degree programs for that kind of work. I could be an exercise physiologist specializing in cardiac rehabilitation."

"That sounds amazing. Why didn't you tell me before?"

"I wasn't sure of the timing of it, and I didn't want to tell you the wrong thing. Now I'm sure."

"What made you so sure?"

He shakes his head. "It wasn't just one moment. It was working with your dad, getting closer to you, watching you at work on the truck wearing that crown." He touches my crown.

I smile. "What if I hadn't won? No crown."

He cups my cheek and gives me a quick kiss. "I was heavily leaning in this direction. There's a few good grad schools in the city with exercise physiology programs. I could commute."

I'm so overwhelmed by his gesture I can't speak for a moment. My throat's clogged with emotion, my eyes hot.

"Sloane? Does that sound okay to you?"

I throw my arms around him. "Yes. Of course it does." I pull back. "Are you sure?"

"One hundred percent."

We gaze into each other's eyes, smiling for a long moment.

"I love you," I say, nearly bursting with it.

He wipes a tear from my cheek, his voice husky. "I love you too."

I take a deep shaky breath. "Wow. It's been such a whirlwind today. I've been so worried about the future, and you kept saying we'd figure it out, but I just didn't see how. You know I never wanted to hold you back, but this sounds like a good choice for you. I think you'll be great at rehab. Your patients will thrive just like Dad. He's getting more energy by the day."

"Speaking of, I hope you don't mind that I invited your dad to join us here."

"What? When did you do that?"

"Here at the reception. When you were talking to Kayla earlier, I pulled Max aside and asked him to drive your dad here. I didn't want you to worry about your dad driving." He gestures toward the entrance of the room.

There's Dad, walking in with Max. Dad dressed nice in a blue button-down shirt and gray trousers. I stand abruptly, wanting to go to him, but Dad gestures for me to stay where I am. He wants me to stay on my throne and do the queen thing. I can't believe Max went along with this. Dad still has two days left of his recommended rest time. He looks steady though, walking with Max to a table close to the dance floor and taking a seat.

I turn back to Caleb. "You think he's okay? He still has two days of prescribed rest."

"I called him after I talked to Max, and your dad assured me he could handle sitting for an hour at a reception for his only daughter."

Wow. Caleb's like part of my inner circle now, working with Dad and Max. I like it.

I elbow him. "Guess you're not jealous of Max anymore. Now the two of you are working as a team."

He chucks me under the chin. "Look at me, I'm growing."

After the dinner service, Audrey approaches our head

table, holding a wireless microphone. "We're going to start the dancing part of the evening. King and queen get the first dance. Any chance you know how to ballroom dance?"

My eyes widen, horrified. "No."

"I can waltz," Caleb says. "Don't worry, I'll lead."

"Awesome!" Audrey says. She clinks a spoon against a glass to get everyone's attention and then announces the first royal dance.

My cheeks flush. It almost feels like we're the bride and groom, sitting at the head table, everyone congratulating us, getting the first dance.

The music starts, "It Had to be You" sung by Harry Connick Jr.

Caleb offers his hand, guiding me off the dais. Dad watches, looking proud. I give him a little wave and follow Caleb onto the dance floor. He takes the lead, one hand holding mine, the other hand on the center of my back, guiding me with him. It's surprisingly easy to follow along. I never thought I was much of a dancer before.

I glance around; all eyes are on us. Dad's smiling. I smile back. He really seems okay.

Caleb leads me in a slow twirl and brings me back. We meet up close, our gazes colliding. My throat clogs with emotion. I just love him so much. He continues the dance, making a slow circular route around the dance floor.

When the song ends, we're near Dad's table.

"Congratulations, Sloane," Dad says. "The crown suits you. You too, Caleb."

I touch my crown. "I'm still getting used to all this. It was a huge surprise."

Dad points over my shoulder.

I turn, and Caleb is down on one knee, holding up a round diamond engagement ring. My hand flies to my mouth.

Audrey rushes over with the microphone, giving it to Caleb. I glance around in shock. Everyone's smiling at us. Several people are taking video with their phones.

I turn back to Caleb. One look at his sincere expression and tears well in my eyes.

"Sloane, I bought this ring after our first date. Thunderbolt hit and that was it for me. You are the coolest, kindest, most beautiful woman I've ever met. I love you more every day, and I will for the rest of my life. Will you marry me?"

I nod through a haze of tears, smiling. "Yes, yes. So much yes." He slides the ring on my finger and pulls me close.

The applause and cheers are so loud I can't even say a word. I go on tiptoe to whisper directly in his ear, hoping he can hear me, "I love you so, so much. You're the best thing to ever happen to me."

He kisses my cheek. "I love you too. I always knew you were the One." He swings me around, making me laugh, and then sets me down.

People crowd the dance floor to congratulate us. I get a flashback to the first time I talked to Caleb when Jenna and Eli got engaged and everyone rushed them. I was a little envious, and now it's happening to me. His brothers and sister hug me and welcome me to the family. I'm on the inside, part of the big happy family that I've always wanted.

"Dad!"

He's at the back of the group surrounding us. "Excuse me," I say, making my way over to him.

He brings me into his arms and hugs me, stroking my hair. "My girl, a queen and soon to be a wife."

I lift my head. "Don't forget I'm your partner. That's a real highlight too."

"Absolutely." He turns and offers his hand to Caleb, who just appeared by my side. "Congrats and welcome to our little family."

Caleb gives him a hug. "Thank you. I'd love to introduce you to my family too. Your family just got a little bigger. And maybe one day you'll have grandkids. Sloane and I both want kids."

Dad's eyes water, his cheeks reddening. "I'm blown away. My daughter's a queen, a wife, and now you're talking about grandkids?"

"Are you feeling okay, Dad? Is it too much for your heart?"

He puts a hand over his heart. "It's exactly what this old heart needs."

I hug him tight around the middle, so happy he's here for the next part of my life. He kisses my hair.

"Can I get your picture for the *Summerdale Sheet*?" a woman asks.

I pull away to face her. "Of course!"

It's Nora Shire, a red-haired woman in her thirties, the sole person left on the newspaper's staff. She smiles. "It's major news when our first king and queen get engaged."

She takes our picture on the dance floor and then has us go up to the dais for more pictures. A crowd gathers, and it seems everyone's taking our picture sitting on our thrones. I hold up my ring hand to show it off. I don't mind pictures so much now as Summerdale's ambassador. There's a larger purpose here. We're part of Summerdale's future.

Finally, after everyone's done taking pictures, the music starts again. Another slow song.

Caleb takes my hand. "We have to dance as an engaged couple now."

"Sure, why not? Are we going to waltz again?"

"This time I want to hold you closer than that."

We reach the dance floor and start a slow sway. It feels so good to be held in his arms. More couples join in. I wave at Jenna and Eli. They're back from their honeymoon in the Caribbean. Jenna points at her ring finger and mouths, *Wow*. Caleb did give me a big sparkly diamond. I smile.

Wyatt and Sydney are dancing, talking animatedly nearby. Adam and Kayla are quiet, gazing into each other's eyes. Even Dad got out here, dancing with Mrs. Ellis. He's always given her a secret senior citizen discount on car repairs. She denies being a senior citizen, despite being in her eighties, so he just takes it off the bill without mentioning it.

I look around for Max. He should be out here too since he did so much to help plan it. He's standing over by the drinks table, looking across the room. I follow his gaze to Brooke, who's sitting alone. I wonder where her fiancé is. You'd think she'd invite him to something like this.

"You believe me now, don't you?" Caleb whispers in my ear. "About the thunderbolt."

"I thought you were a little nuts at first, but this is one more for the Robinson family legend."

He dips me, and I squeak in surprise. "Sure is." He pulls me back up. "I just want you to know, no matter what my travel schedule looks like this year, I'll always make time for us. You are the center my world revolves around."

I swallow over the lump of emotion in my throat. "Gah, you're going to make me cry. Thank you for saying that, but I'm not worried anymore. We've got a plan that works for both of us."

"One day you'll be telling our grandkids how you turned down my offer to buy you a drink the first time we met."

"And you'll be telling them about the thunderbolt that made you propose marriage on our first date."

He kisses me. "Tonight was my first real proposal. Before I was just informing you of the facts."

"So cocky."

"I am the king."

"I still can't believe I'm the queen *and* I'm engaged. What a crazy wonderful night!"

"Get ready for a crazy wonderful life."

I beam and hug him tight. With Caleb's bold predictions, I believe with all of my heart.

EPILOGUE

Two months later...

Spring is here with all the new beginnings of life and a lot of new beginnings around Summerdale too. I'm sitting in Dad's office at Murray's while they set up stuff in the bay, just pondering all the wonderful changes. All that fundraising for the shelter—along with a large anonymous donation, which could only have come from billionaire Wyatt—means construction will begin soon on Summerdale's state-of-the-art animal shelter. Another new beginning—Wyatt's sisters, Brooke and Paige, bought the old farmhouse on the end of Lovers' Lane and plan to open a bed and breakfast.

But the best new beginning is what's happening right now.

"Ready for you, Sloane," the director says, poking his head in the office.

That's right. I have my own reality show on the Turbo channel called *The Right Fix*. I fix cars and teach people at home how I do it. The perfect combination of my natural talents—cars and teaching. I wasn't looking to be on TV; it found me thanks to a video that went viral—me dressed as Queen Snowflake, climbing down from the stalled truck, fixing it, and going back to my throne. Probably helps that we have our own homegrown famous actress, Harper Ellis, with major connections. She approached me with the idea, I ran it by Dad, who was surprisingly enthusiastic, and it was a go.

Today's our third taping, and I'm pretty comfortable with how it works. The great thing is, Dad *loves* it. He's on the show with me, but more in a supporting role. He says work is fun for him again, and he never wants to retire. If this show takes off, I can expand with another bay and more mechanics. That means Dad could at least have the *option* to retire. We'll see.

I step into place at my workbench with the pieces of a carburetor laid out already with my tools. Lights go up, camera lenses focus in, the director gives the cue, and I get in the zone. Time flies as I work.

We take five, and I'm barely aware time has passed. Then it's time to shift over to a newer car, a Toyota Corolla, so I can demonstrate an oil change. Simple maintenance tasks like this aren't exciting for me, but are helpful to people who didn't grow up in a garage like I did. I've also done segments on changing your own air filter and how to know when you need new tires.

Taping ends, and the crew packs up. I sense someone staring and look out to the parking lot. Caleb's leaning against his car in his leather jacket and jeans, smiling at me. He's proud of my work.

I let out a happy sigh as he approaches. The love of my life.

I meet him halfway, and he grabs me in a monster hug that lifts me off the ground.

He gives me a quick kiss. "You're a natural."

"It does feel right."

He sets me down and frames my face with both hands, leaning in for a tender kiss. I melt against him. The kiss turns deeper as the fire ignites between us. A long moment later, we come up for air, gazing into each other's eyes. The love is a palpable thing, binding us together. My man. We plan to get married in a small ceremony this summer.

Ya know, they should change that story about the ugly duckling. Sometimes you have to be the odd duck to own your inner queen.

Don't miss the next book in the series, *Blazing*, where Max refuses to get involved with his biggest client. He didn't count on Brooke crossing the line first!

Max

I'm determined to grow my landscape design business fast. It's the only way to save the home that's been in our family for generations. So when I land my biggest client ever, the new inn with a huge property, I know better than to get involved with the sexy owner. Besides, Brooke Winters is engaged, and I can't risk stirring up drama in the small community I depend on for my business.

Brooke

Have you ever had such bad luck with guys that you start wearing your sister's old engagement ring as an anti-man shield? Just me? Anyway, it's working and good thing too. I can't afford a distraction when I'm the lead architect for the old farmhouse my sister and I plan to turn into an inn. Everything's on the line, including our life savings. We have to open on time or lose our shirts.

Only I didn't count on a gorgeous landscaper brightening every chaotic day with his distracting warm smile. Even my dog is in love with Max. I'm made of sterner stuff. Until I impulsively kiss him and—

Fireworks. I didn't know they were a real thing.

Now I'm navigating a slippery slope, desperately trying to put up professional boundaries all while keeping our renovation project on schedule. This will either go down in a blaze of glory or a blazing hot mess.

ALSO BY KYLIE GILMORE

Unleashed Romance <<steamy romcoms with dogs!

Fetching (Book 1)

Dashing (Book 2)

Sporting (Book 3)

Toying (Book 4)

Blazing (Book 5)

Chasing (Book 6)

Daring (Book 7)

Leading (Book 8)

Racing (Book 9)

Loving (Book 10)

The Clover Park Series <<brothers who put family first!

The Opposite of Wild (Book 1)

Daisy Does It All (Book 2)

Bad Taste in Men (Book 3)

Kissing Santa (Book 4)

Restless Harmony (Book 5)

Not My Romeo (Book 6)

Rev Me Up (Book 7)

An Ambitious Engagement (Book 8)

Clutch Player (Book 9)

A Tempting Friendship (Book 10)

Clover Park Bride: Nico and Lily's Wedding

A Valentine's Day Gift (Book 11)

Maggie Meets Her Match (Book 12)

The Clover Park STUDS series <<hawt geeks who unleash into studs!

Almost Over It (Book 1)

Almost Married (Book 2)

Almost Fate (Book 3)

Almost in Love (Book 4)

Almost Romance (Book 5)

Almost Hitched (Book 6)

Happy Endings Book Club Series <<the Campbell family and a romance book club collide!

Hidden Hollywood (Book 1)

Inviting Trouble (Book 2)

So Revealing (Book 3)

Formal Arrangement (Book 4)

Bad Boy Done Wrong (Book 5)

Mess With Me (Book 6)

Resisting Fate (Book 7)

Chance of Romance (Book 8)

Wicked Flirt (Book 9)

An Inconvenient Plan (Book 10)

A Happy Endings Wedding (Book 11)

The Rourkes Series <<swoonworthy princes and kickass princesses!

Royal Catch (Book 1)

Royal Hottie (Book 2)

Royal Darling (Book 3)

Royal Charmer (Book 4)

Royal Player (Book 5)

Royal Shark (Book 6)

Rogue Prince (Book 7)

Rogue Gentleman (Book 8)

Rogue Rascal (Book 9)

Rogue Angel (Book 10)

Rogue Devil (Book 11)

Rogue Beast (Book 12)

Check out my website for the most up-to-date list of my books:
kyliegilmore.com/books

ABOUT THE AUTHOR

Kylie Gilmore is the *USA Today* bestselling author of the Unleashed Romance series, the Rourkes series, the Happy Endings Book Club series, the Clover Park series, and the Clover Park STUDS series. She writes humorous romance that makes you laugh, cry, and reach for a cold glass of water.

Kylie lives in New York with her family, two cats, and a nutso dog. When she's not writing, reading hot romance, or dutifully taking notes at writing conferences, you can find her flexing her muscles all the way to the high cabinet for her secret chocolate stash.

Sign up for Kylie's Newsletter and get a FREE book! kyliegilmore.com/newsletter

For text alerts on Kylie's new releases, text KYLIE to the number 21000. (US only)

For more fun stuff check out Kylie's website https://www.kyliegilmore.com.

Thanks for reading *Toying.* I hope you enjoyed it. Would you like to know about new releases? You can sign up for my new release email list at kyliegilmore.com/newsletter. I promise not to clog your inbox! Only new release info, sales, and some fun giveaways.

I love to hear from readers! You can find me at:
    kyliegilmore.com
    Instagram.com/kyliegilmore
    Facebook.com/KylieGilmoreToo
    Twitter @KylieGilmoreToo

If you liked Caleb and Sloane's story, please leave a review on your favorite retailer's website or Goodreads. Thank you.

Made in the USA
Monee, IL
26 August 2021

76601646R00115